The Persistence of Fate

a novel

C.R.C.

RIVER GROVE
BOOKS

Published by River Grove Books
Austin, TX
www.rivergrovebooks.com

Distributed by River Grove Books

Design and composition by Greenleaf Book Group and Mimi Bark
Cover design by Greenleaf Book Group and Mimi Bark
Cover images used under license from ©Shutterstock.com/mamita

Publisher's Cataloging-in-Publication data is available.

Print ISBN: 978-1-63299-446-2

eBook ISBN: 978-1-63299-447-9

First Edition

To all the soulful souls who look past
life's monotony, seeing beyond the veil of illusion
and daring to question everything

From the moment we are born
We have an inner compass
That guides us to little hints and signs
For us to discover, to follow
Putting us in the right place
At the right time
It is Fate, whispering
Leading us to our calling
To our higher selves,
Along the way Delivering us to our personal destiny
Where we must fulfill what was left undone.
It isn't always the easiest path to follow
But the journey pushes us to a greater Awakening.

Prologue

Have you ever wondered what lies beyond this material world? Even beyond death? Most people subscribe to the belief that we die and go to Heaven, or that we die and wait for Jesus's second coming to be resurrected from our graves. There are others who believe that we just die and that is all there is to it. Whatever you choose to believe, this story may challenge your preexisting beliefs on life and death. Or it may simply make you ponder the possibilities of this realm we live in. It might even evoke the question: What more is there to this thing we call life? One question begs another.

Many people, when asked what they think the meaning of life is, will answer that it is love. Love is intoxicating. Those who fear it want it the most. Yet they sabotage themselves by running away before ever even giving themselves the chance to love and to be loved in return. Perhaps they're afraid of being hurt, so they put up excuses and walls instead of opening themselves up to the love they crave. With well-thought-out rationality, they will do whatever it takes to talk themselves out of the very love they are starving for.

There is no rationality in love—none. Your heart falls for someone, and it consumes your very soul. It will kill you if you fight it, slowly and painfully, every day that you and your beloved are apart. Love doesn't care if you come from privilege and royalty or if you're dirt poor, what society deems a "nobody." The universal energies say that like attracts like, and that is true, but there are also complementary opposites that attract each other. In those cases, one has something the other needs to have balance in their life. Many of us, born into certain cultures and places in the world, are taught certain beliefs, morals, and values that we must live by and uphold. As children, we don't second-guess what our parents and family in general teach us. As we grow older and start to discover the world for ourselves, our mind and our spirit begin to realize just how much we don't know and how much more there is out there to be discovered. Love teaches us that no matter how different two people are—in their backgrounds, social status, race, or inward and outward differences—there's no obstacle that the power of love cannot overcome.

This is what two young people from completely different worlds—Emery and Rose, once known as Emmett and Helena—discover in this story of love, fate, and the power of free will. They decide for themselves if the seductive allure of history and familiarity between two souls is worth the resurfacing of old wounds, and although it may be painful, they grow in the process. Growth—to evolve from old and outdated behaviors that no longer serve any purpose—is something to strive for. If growth is resisted, one is doomed to repeat past mistakes.

Time and distance cannot keep two people apart if fate wills that they be together. Our destiny is already written before we are even born to our parents. It's that little voice that guides us throughout life; we must always listen to it and trust it. It is our road map to our fate. It can be those instinctual feelings we get sometimes but dismiss in our daily lives. Sometimes those feelings can be about small things; other times they involve monumental decisions that could change our direction forever.

We all have our course set; we must keep an open mind when traveling along our journey, knowing that all will be okay, especially when going through the challenges that may present themselves. They are there to make us grow and evolve from who we used to be to who we are meant to become.

A unique young couple experiences this for themselves along their journey in search of meaning. They discover a simple truth that stares us all in the face. Love is the meaning of life. Loving one another makes life worth living. It makes us become better versions of ourselves. Both in search of something more, they experience for themselves the persistence of fate.

Emery

Chapter 1

"Why did you invite them?" Emery asks his mother, annoyed that his parents invited Juliet, an overzealous admirer of his, to dinner that night. Standing behind his mother's dressing table, Emery continues to grumble. "I don't want to sit there and be fake, pretending like I actually *want* to be there. Or as if I even fancy the girl. Really, Mother. It's not fair to either of us! She gets her hopes up even if I simply look her way." Emery crosses his arms in defiance. He knows he can't get out of the commitment, and he's angry that his mother has put him in this position.

Victoria Williams looks at her son through her vanity mirror, her large blue eyes emphasized by the champagne color of her eyeshadow. "Emery, she is simply accompanying her parents to dinner. That is all. You don't have to speak to her if you don't want to. Just keep to yourself. And they will be here shortly, so go get dressed!"

Emery Williams was born into a wealthy English family, with roots dating all the way back to the eighteenth century. His biggest concern is doing his best not to behave out of character for someone of his family name. Though he comes from privileged circumstances, his life isn't entirely easy, as he has one looming struggle: He wants to be himself, and he doesn't want to be forced to marry for money instead of love. Of course, he knows his struggles don't compare at all to the kinds of real-world struggles so many other people have—trying to put food on the table, feed children, pay rent, and sometimes care for elderly parents.

But it is a real struggle. At age thirty-four, he wants to be free from the expectations of his world of titles and class. He enjoys the lifestyle and carefree luxury money allows him, especially from his rolling family estate in Virginia Water, Surrey, just forty minutes from downtown London. But the fame and gossip—and the constant watchful and judgmental public eye—he could do without.

He could also do without the admirers who, he is pretty sure, pursue him because of his position, not to mention his wealth. Emery is also one of the most eligible bachelors in all of England. Women flock to him and will come around just to catch a glimpse of him. His mother's friends all hope that one of their daughters will someday end up with Emery. However, he is distant and unavailable. On the surface, it seems that distance is due to his career as an archaeologist, which demands a lot of travel. His studies allow him to escape the world he sees as superficial and silly. Emery is much more interested in things that have depth and mystery, but he also is glad to have an excuse to escape *her*—Juliet, the very persistent daughter of his mother's friend—who will be arriving any minute.

Emery, arms still crossed, eyes still fixed on his mother's eyes in the dressing table mirror, shakes his head. "You know I have no choice."

Victoria raises her eyebrows, gifts him a little smile, and shrugs. She checks her makeup one more time and heads out the door, but she stops to look back at Emery.

"Oh, and, dear, please try not to start a debate with your father while our guests are over. You two just don't know when to stop once you start." Then she closes the bedroom door behind her.

Emery's relationship with his father is fairly good, even though the only thing they agree on is that the sky is blue. Sir Ashby and Emery often enter into fierce debates at the dinner table over the Catholic Church and the basic structures of religion—so much so that some guests feel uncomfortable in the midst of such a conversation. To be honest, they both enjoy the drama.

But more important right now than his father's drama is Emery's frustration at having to show up—yet again—to an event where he will be forced to endure the attentions of a woman he isn't interested in. He wants love, but he wants to find it on his own terms, the way his friends did. All of Emery's friends have a beloved or are about to get married; they are ready to settle down. He would never say it aloud to anyone, but his mother, Victoria, whom he has a very close and intuitive bond with, says that the only reason his friends' parents approve of the marriages and relationships is the wealth and status of the girls' families. He often tells his mother how if he married, he would want it to be for love and nothing else. She believes in allowing Emery to be himself and does not argue with him when he speaks of the importance of marrying for love rather than status.

His mother is incredibly spiritual. She believes in reincarnation, past lives, and the law of the universe. She also believes in metaphysics and has the gifts of clairvoyance and claircognizance—the gift of psychic knowledge. She will sometimes go to church with Ashby to show support or simply accompany him so that he doesn't have to go alone. Victoria is kind like that.

Emery is much like his mother; he has a certain type of wisdom that seems unusual for a man of his age to possess. She knows him better than anyone, yet for some reason it seems as if her favorite pastime is to revel in his suffering. Often he hears her giggling quietly when she sees him trying to escape the attentions of Juliet or any other young lady who wants to date him. He is so polite and well-mannered that he can't imagine insulting any of the women by turning them down. It would also cause a bit of an uncomfortable rift between the families, so he thinks it best to avoid giving a direct answer and instead focus on finding a way around the situation.

Emery knows that his mother has always hoped and wished for him to find love for himself, someone who will be good to him and love him for who he is, not for what he has. But she also understands that he will have a hard time trusting completely and letting someone in, because of his fear of the other person being with him simply for superficial reasons. Luckily, Emery is very intuitive and can see right through people. He can see what drives them, their insecurities and faults.

Emery glares at the back of his mother as she walks away. Defeated, he walks slowly to his own bedroom, almost dragging his feet. He really has no choice but to make the best of the evening. It is not just about honor but also about treating people with dignity. Emery is extremely compassionate with everyone, for he knows all too well that a little bit of kindness and love can go a long way, for anyone in general. People remember for the rest of their lives the way someone treated them, and no matter how short of an interaction he has with someone, he always wants to leave a good impression. Some people in London get caught up in reading tabloids and the papers, making judgments about his character based on lies. It would be exhausting and too much for anyone to bear after a while. However, he has learned to deal with it, thanks in part to his mother's help.

He can hear Juliet's family arriving on the gravel driveway below his bedroom window, as well as his parents walking outside to greet them. He peeks out the window to catch a glimpse of the activity. Juliet looks up just then and sees him; she smiles. Frantically, he darts off to the side of the window, out of view. He isn't quite ready to face her, to politely but firmly turn away her advances.

Emery rushes to shower and get dressed; he expects his mother's knock at the door soon, insisting he come down and join them. After getting out of the shower, and just as expected, he hears a knock at the door. He quickly ties his oversized white bath robe at the waist and shouts, "Coming!" while hastily opening the door.

But instead of his mother, it is Nannie, the housekeeper, a very sweet woman who has worked for his family for nearly fifty years. Her large dark eyes look up at him in astonishment.

"Master Em," she says affectionately, "your mother would be unnerved to see you are not ready to join them for dinner. They have already been seated at the dinner table, sir."

Emery pushes his black hair back and nods. "Thank you, Nannie. I'll be down as soon as I can."

Emery quickly closes the door and rushes to get dressed. He chooses a simple yet elegant outfit and heads downstairs.

Upon Emery entering the dining room, Juliet stands up, apparently out of nervousness, thus creating a very awkward scene at the dinner table. Juliet's parents look at her with puzzlement. Of course, Victoria knows about Juliet being smitten with Emery—everybody seems to know it. As she sips her wine, she tries to hide her mischievous grin behind her wine glass.

Emery moves to sit beside his father, but seeing Juliet sitting so close to Sir Ashby, he realizes that it is too close to her for comfort. He chooses to sit beside his mother at the other end of the table.

"So sorry to join you late," he says apologetically.

"It's quite all right, Emery. We only just sat down," Mr. Montgomery says. He smiles affectionately at Emery from across the table. Jack Montgomery and his wife, Elizabeth Martin Montgomery, are lifelong friends of Emery's parents. Growing up in the same social circles, they would have had a difficult time avoiding each other. They went to all the same schools, parties, and gatherings.

Elizabeth Montgomery is clearly very fond of Emery and deeply wants him to become her son-in-law. She knows Emery is not all that interested in her Juliet, but she doesn't really care. She probably hopes he'll come around eventually, once he realizes how hard it is to find someone else of his class and intelligence worth marrying.

It is well known that Elizabeth Montgomery is prejudiced against people who are not of her class. She deems them unworthy of conversation even! She isn't a very nice woman, to say the very least. Emery has come to the conclusion that Mrs. Montgomery is narrow-minded and stuck in the Stone Age with her way of thinking. She set her sights on him marrying her daughter from the moment he was born; Juliet was born three months after Emery.

Victoria doesn't agree with the way Elizabeth thinks—with all of her snobbery and prejudice; the two women actually grew apart even as girls. But Emery figures she puts up with Elizabeth because Ashby is such good friends with Jack.

Conversation at the dinner table gets off to a lively start, with Jack Montgomery probing Emery about his newest archaeological finds.

"So, I hear that they found another tomb in Egypt. Were you a part of that expedition?" he asks Emery in between sips of his soup.

Emery puts down his spoon and napkin. "I was, initially," he says. "I assisted with some of the first excavations, and once we knew what we had found, someone else took over."

Mrs. Montgomery fakes interest as she widens her eyes at Emery. "Why did you not continue?"

"I had been there for quite some time, and I was due to come home anyway. The site is in very good hands with the people who took over." Emery can see the pretentiousness seeping through Mrs. Montgomery's pores. She doesn't care one bit about what he does; nor does she care about his interests or passions. All she wants is for him to marry Juliet so that the two families' banking and financing business empires can merge through their marriage. Emery also figures she wants to be able to say—to boast to others, actually—that she is a part of the "Williams family."

But such a marriage will *never* happen—not if Emery has a choice in the matter. And he *does* have a choice, doesn't he?

As the dinner continues, Ashby invites Mr. Montgomery to attend church with him and Victoria on Sunday. As his father extends the invitation, Emery quietly looks down at his dinner plate. He hopes it isn't something he will be forced to attend too for the sake of being polite. He hates church; his father knows very well where he stands on organized religion—and the two of them see things very differently. Emery's views are more in agreement with those of his mother. He is very angry and upset at the fact that his father continues to be a part of the Catholic Church, an organization that allows for young children to be hurt and abused by Catholic priests. The church doesn't hold the priests accountable for their actions by ensuring they are—every last one of them—brought to justice.

"Yeah, go ahead and support the abuse of innocent children," Emery mutters under his breath.

Emery's mother goes red from embarrassment. "Emery, now is not the time," she pleads in a whisper.

Sir Ashby stares angrily at his son. "I am not supporting the abuse of young boys! This is my faith," he hits back assertively. "I follow what the Bible says. I just go to hear the sermon."

"How can you say that? That you 'just go to hear the sermon'?" Emery fires back as he angrily stares down his father. "Just because it isn't happening to you or anyone you know doesn't mean that it isn't happening. It's almost as if you don't care about those children. Clearly you revel in your privilege, Father."

The energy at the table shifts to an uncomfortable silence.

Emery loves his father but also resents his authoritarian "I know best" attitude toward him. In that silence the resentment builds. Eventually, everything Emery doesn't say will come bursting out, sooner rather than later. He won't be controlled by his family's expectations and traditions. He won't. Emery will do things his way, regardless of whether his father approves or not. Ever since he was a little boy, he was made aware that he was held to a different standard than some of his peers. It made him feel isolated and trapped.

The day is coming soon when he will no longer be able to avoid the mounting expectations heaped on him by his family. But even worse, he dreads moving forward without feeling true love. What is a man without a partner to share life with, to enjoy the beauty of sunrises with, to discuss the day's events in the evening, to hold as he falls asleep at night?

If only his father knew how Emery felt about all of the expectations placed on him—from the family name to marrying sweet but uninteresting Juliet. What his father sees as Emery's birthright, Emery sees as a death sentence.

And a very lonely one at that.

Chapter 2

"Emery!" Victoria interjects.

"No, Mother! I will not be silenced!" Emery snaps back. "What if it happened to *me*?" he asks his father, his ocean-blue eyes glaring angrily at Sir Ashby.

Mr. Williams's face grows stern.

"If it happened to me, you wouldn't be going to that place you call a 'church,' with its man-made rules," Emery continues.

Before his father can say something back, Emery excuses himself from the table to get some fresh air.

Victoria apologizes on behalf of Emery and abruptly follows after him. She walks out to the garden, where Emery is angrily walking through the rose bushes.

"Emery!" she calls out to him.

Emery turns to look at her, still upset. "Yes?" he reluctantly asks.

Mrs. Williams lifts her dress a bit as she steps onto the gravel. "Was that necessary? Going off like that on your father at the dinner table? What was it that I asked of you before dinner?"

Emery runs his hands through his dark hair and looks up to the sky, letting out a slight sigh before answering. "Mother, you know how I feel about him attending church every Sunday, as well as him still being a part of *that* religion. It's wrong! Why can't you see that? You of all people should understand," Emery says with bitterness.

Mrs. Williams crosses her arms and affectionately gazes at him. "Emery, I understand your views and feelings about this subject. I truly do. But you must understand, it is not so much the religion itself that is doing this to young boys. These are the actions of wicked men; this is *their* doing and theirs alone. The faith itself is not bad. Your father wholeheartedly believes in the Catholic faith. He is heartbroken about what goes on and that these men get away with it! He is upset about it too—"

"Well, he damn well has a funny way of showing it, by going every Sunday and donating money!" Emery shouts angrily, interrupting his mother. "Does he know what his money funds? It funds the church's ability to move these priests to other locations. It allows for them to get away with it. Don't you see that?"

Mrs. Williams sighs in exhaustion. She rests her hands on Emery's shoulders. "I understand that. I will talk to him about no longer donating money and maybe taking some sort of action to stop this. Maybe there is a way? I'm sure of it. Whatever it is, we will figure it out. I promise," she says, trying to reassure him.

Emery looks at his mother, a bit more at ease. "I apologize for my outburst. I am sorry. I disregarded what you asked of me, so I apologize," he says sincerely.

Mrs. Williams smiles. "Yeah, well, you know I'm not the only one you have to apologize to. The Montgomerys are still in there. I'm sure they've moved over to the cigar and brandy room. The men anyway," she adds.

"Yeah. I will apologize to them too," Emery says reluctantly as he takes his mother's arm and gently wraps it around him. "Come on, you can come with me."

They've begun making their way back inside when Mrs. Williams turns to Emery and says, "You know, Juliet is probably terrified of you now, knowing you're capable of such passionate anger." She laughs as she teases Emery.

He simply looks down at the ground, annoyed. "I don't care. I hope it scared her off. Maybe she will leave me alone," he says, truly hoping she would.

"Your father is probably onto you. I bet he's thinking right now that you did it on purpose to scare her off." Victoria giggles.

As they reenter the house, they find Juliet standing in the living room waiting for them.

"Is everything all right?" Juliet asks both Emery and his mother.

Emery and his mother exchange a glance before answering.

"Uh, yeah, no . . . everything is fine. Yeah," Emery says awkwardly.

Mrs. Williams smiles at both Juliet and Emery before excusing herself. "I'll leave you two. I have to go join Mrs. Montgomery. I'm sure she's wondering where I am." She looks at Emery with a mischievous grin.

He tries to ignore her and leave the room, but Juliet isn't giving up anytime soon.

"Are you leaving?" she asks. "You haven't spoken to me all evening, Emery. Have I done something?"

Emery stops before heading out the door, taken aback by Juliet's forwardness. "Uh, no, not at all. I just . . . umm . . . I'm just tired and want to go to bed." Emery struggles to come up with a good excuse to leave, but Juliet doesn't make it easy.

"I haven't seen you in a long time, Em. I really would love it if you spent some time with me. Maybe play something for us?" she says as she points at the grand piano in the living room. She gazes at Emery with what seems to him to be a look of intense longing. "Please?" she begs.

Emery sighs and walks over to the piano, and Juliet smiles happily.

"What do you want me to play?" Emery asks, doing his best not to sound annoyed.

"Anything! Your favorite song? Or whatever is easiest," Juliet says joyously. She seems beside herself to have even just a moment alone with him.

Emery begins to play a song his mother used to play for him when he was a child and just learning how to play the piano. She wrote it for him, as she loves music and plays the piano often.

Juliet sits beside Emery and listens as he plays. She stares at him as he furrows his brow with concentration. In what feels like a sudden move, she leans toward his lips and kisses him. She continues kissing him, not seeming to care that he isn't kissing her back.

Emery pulls away. "Juliet!" he exclaims.

She doesn't listen but continues pushing herself onto him, trying to reconnect with a kiss. Emery grabs both her hands and pulls them off his face and neck.

"Juliet! Stop!" he says angrily. "What is the matter with you?" He moves away from the piano.

"Do you really not know? Emery, I've been in love with you from the moment I first saw you. We were just children then, but

I've always loved you," Juliet exclaims, pouring out her feelings as though she doesn't care if she makes a fool of herself.

Emery scowls at her, upset and disappointed at her actions.

"Juliet, I love you—" he begins.

"I knew it!" she says without letting him finish. She throws herself at him, trying to kiss him again.

"Juliet!" Emery raises his voice. The veins in his neck appear as he becomes far more enraged. He clenches his jaw and grips Juliet fiercely, moving her away from his body. He finishes his sentence with "As a friend."

Juliet begins to cry, her chest heaving, at Emery's rejection. After a moment, as though embarrassed at what a fool she has made of herself, Juliet does her best to pull herself together. "Is there someone else?" she asks, looking at Emery with tears in her eyes.

"No. Juliet, I'm just not interested. I see you as nothing more than a friend. Please understand this: I don't mean to hurt you." Emery knows he needs to be as honest and gentle with her as he can be, no matter how hard that felt just then.

Juliet visibly struggles to hold herself together. "All right. . . . I understand," she says, looking utterly crushed.

She collects herself before joining Mrs. Williams and her mother in the grand living room. Emery takes a deep breath and runs up the stairs quickly before he can be seen by anyone else.

Emery gets up to his room and locks the door behind him. Before falling asleep, he decides to do some light reading in hopes of getting his mind off of what just occurred with Juliet. He picks up a book he's been looking forward to reading. Sent to him by a publisher in the United States, the book—titled *What Lies Beyond Us*—deals with reincarnation and past lives and is set in a seaside town in Northern California called Carmel-by-the-Sea. According to the publisher, the book has been a huge hit in the States.

Emery loves hearing stories about past lives and anything to do with mysterious topics and unseen forces at work in people's lives. The book was written by a therapist who practices past-life regressions on her patients—patients who wish to uncover phobias and other unexplainable blockages they are experiencing in their lives. The author even has scientific proof that past lives are real. Whatever sort of evidence the therapist presents in the book, Emery relishes every bit of it.

As the night wears on, he keeps reading and finishes the book easily, finding it incredibly fascinating—so much so that he looks up at the clock and is shocked to see that it is one in the morning; the hours just flew by.

He puts his robe on and heads downstairs. It is quiet, and almost all the lights are off—except in one room, his father's study.

Emery drags himself over there to apologize to his father for his behavior earlier that evening. He stops at the open door and knocks.

Mr. Williams looks up from where he's sitting and signals for Emery to have a seat. He proceeds to put his glass of brandy down and rests his elbows on the desk in front of him.

"To what do I owe this great pleasure," he says in a tired and sarcastic tone.

Emery sits down on the chair in front of his father. "I saw you were still up and wanted to apologize for the way I acted earlier at dinner. I didn't mean to embarrass you in any way. I am sorry."

Mr. Williams looks down at his brandy and back at Emery. "Want some? Grab a glass," he says calmly.

Emery helps himself to a bit of his father's brandy.

Mr. Williams answers, "You didn't embarrass me."

Emery glances at his father, confused.

"You didn't embarrass me, not one bit. I have to say I am proud you have such strong views and are passionate about others' suffering. You care about people genuinely, and that makes you a great man, more than I ever could be. And I acknowledge that—"

"Dad, you're a great man," Emery interrupts.

Mr. Williams raises his hand gently, signaling for Emery to let him finish. "I haven't always been. . . . I have grown as a person immensely ever since you came into my life as a baby. You've taught me a great deal about being mindful and doing my best to not get caught up in the bubble that is our world."

Mr. Williams continues, "I've given a lot of thought to what you said to me at the dinner table, and I have decided that I shall practice my faith privately and no longer attend mass. I will also take political action in hopes of holding those men who commit these crimes accountable for their horrific actions. . . . It is time I start doing the right thing instead of turning a blind eye like the rest of the world does."

Emery puts his glass down on the desk. A giant smile of contentment forms across his face. "Thank you, Dad! I'm serious—thank you for listening and doing this. Thank you for taking a stand."

Mr. Williams gives him a warm smile back and stands to give Emery a big hug. "No need to thank me. Thank you for making me see reason. I love you." He starts embracing Emery tightly.

Emery is beaming with happiness and pride that his words and feelings got through to his father, who is easily one of the most powerful men in England. For him to take action against something like this is a big deal. People will listen to him and hopefully follow his lead.

They sit around in the office and talk for about thirty more minutes. To Emery's surprise, the conversation takes a slight turn.

"Nannie told me something about you and Juliet having a bit of a quarrel in the living room? Is this true?"

Emery slumps back in his chair. He stares up at the ceiling before answering. His father laughs, as if he knows just what Emery is thinking. *Can anything possibly happen in this bloody household without a living soul knowing about it? The answer, sadly, is no.*

"Oh god! Did Nannie see?" Emery asks.

"I believe so. She said she saw Juliet throwing herself at you. You rejected her, and she overheard Juliet's confession of love for you," Mr. Williams says with a sigh.

"Great!" Emery quips sarcastically. "I didn't even see Nannie! What is she, a ninja?"

Mr. Williams begins to laugh. "She is so stealthy, that Nannie! You don't even hear or see her, but she sees you!"

"I know!" Emery adds. "Can't get away with anything!"

"Well, as you know, son, I only hire the best of the best," Mr. Williams continues, showcasing his charismatic wit. Still laughing to the point of tears, he shakes his head before getting up. "All right, young man. Let's go to bed! Your mother is probably wondering where I am. She's about to send the dogs for me any minute now."

They wrap up their conversation for the night and head off to sleep. Emery is glad he was able to patch things up with his dad after what happened. Sometimes when that very thing occurs during their conversations, days or even weeks go by before they speak. Usually it has a lot to do with the fact that anytime Emery is upset about something, he buries himself in work to get his mind off of it. His father knows and usually lets him be, giving Emery space to cool off. In this case, things turned out better, since Mr. Williams decided to take action against the injustices of the Catholic Church rather than continue to turn a blind eye.

Chapter 3

The following day Emery gets a call from an old friend and fellow archaeologist by the name of Theodore Hartfield. They decide to meet up in London at a local pub that evening. Theodore and Emery have known each other since they were in diapers. They attended the same university together, but after graduating they drifted apart a little. He is getting married over the summer, and the Williams family is invited.

Emery arrives at the pub and is greeted by his friend at the bar. Theodore made sure to find a pub willing to close down for added privacy, as Emery is always hounded by photographers wherever he goes in town.

"Emery Williams! It's been too long, my dear friend, hasn't it?" Theodore says, extending his hand out to Emery. His dazzling white smile lights up the whole room. Theodore looks like a movie star.

Emery smiles. "It has indeed," he answers, pulling Theodore in for a hug. "So, what's going on? What are we drinking?"

"Guinness. As always."

Theodore orders two beers for himself and Emery. They catch up on everything that's been going on since they last saw each other.

Theodore brings up a job he has been contracted to work on. He and his team have been hired to dig around an old abandoned estate nearby, and he asks Emery to join him.

"It's good money," Theodore says to Emery with a smirk.

"You know it's not about the money," Emery replies, taking a sip of his beer.

Theodore rolls his eyes. "No shit. Man, I had to close this fucking pub down for you. I am very aware of who I'm talking to. Mr. Emery Williams, everyone!" he says aloud to the empty bar.

Emery laughs into his pint of beer. "So, what is this for? The museum? Personal?"

"It's a bit of fun to pass the time, you know? I haven't seen you in a while, and I figured we could hang out and get back in touch. Just like the old days. Obviously, now you've become a bit of a recluse, so the only way I can lure you out is to talk about work." Theodore shakes his head. "But I have been hired by someone, and I would love to have you help me."

"Well, I just haven't been feeling all that social. The party and paparazzi scene get old after a while," Emery states, staring down pensively at his beer.

Theodore looks at Emery, and his smile changes to an expression of seriousness and concern. "Are you all right, man? You seem depressed or something. You're exhibiting signs of a breakup. Don't tell me! You and Juliet? Finally?"

"What? No! I mean, something did happen last night, but not what you think . . ."

"What happened?" Theodore asks, this time awaiting Emery's reply without cutting him off with his guesses.

"She confessed her love for me and kissed me repeatedly. It was so awkward." Emery cringes.

"Isn't she really hot? I haven't seen her lately, but I've always thought she was a beautiful girl," Theodore says, looking at Emery with a confused expression.

"She is very beautiful, but there is no connection. I want an emotional and mental connection. You can't force that shit. That's what a lot of people think of me, isn't it? That I must be some superficial prick. It's not true. Juliet definitely buys into the whole image that the world has created for me. I just know she does. I can feel it. And the way she looks at me . . . like some sort of crazed fan."

Theodore listens quietly, letting Emery vent to him. "No, I get you, man. I get it. Most women think that men just want sex, and it's not true. We want love too, you know? That passionate movie type of love! Like *Gone with the Wind*!" Theodore says, causing both him and Emery to burst into laughter.

"I can genuinely say I have missed you and your humor," Emery says, laughing.

"Oh, really? So, you just bullshit everyone else or what?" Theodore asks.

Emery sighs, rolling his eyes at Theodore. "Sometimes, yeah—"

"What? Wow!" Theodore says, teasing.

"What? Don't act like you haven't done it! Lied to someone, I mean, when they say they miss you. . . . I feel bad not saying it back! Like I'll hurt their feelings or something if I don't," Emery says honestly.

Theodore sighs, staring at the TV at the bar. "No, I have done that. But I figure that people do that sort of thing all the time. I don't know. . . . It's stuff you say but you don't really mean . . ." He trails off, as if slightly confused by his own words. "Whatever! Hey, what are you doing after this?"

Emery frowns and takes another sip of his beer. "I don't know. Nothing, I guess. Probably just retire off to my parents' place. Why?"

"I don't know. I mean, I want to keep hanging out, but we can't really go back to my place. My fiancée's parents are in town, and it wouldn't be comfortable," Theodore says, sounding bummed out. "I don't want to stay here that long. Full disclosure, I was only able to close the pub down for about an hour or two . . . and it's been two," Theodore says, laughing.

"We can go back to my parents'. They won't mind. Besides, my mother hasn't seen you in a while. I'm sure she'd be delighted to see you again," Emery says, getting up to pay the tab.

"All right, let's go." Theodore stands up to grab his coat.

They head out of the pub, only to have paparazzi awaiting them the second they open the door. Emery keeps his gaze on the ground and rushes toward his waiting car.

"Jesus!" Theodore mutters under his breath, struggling to follow.

"Back up! Back up!" shouts the doorman assertively to the aggressive photographers. Theodore pushes through and hops into the car after Emery.

"What a nightmare! Wouldn't want to be you," Theodore yells out. "Must be exhausting! Another reason why we shouldn't go to my place. Wouldn't want the circus to follow us, now, would we?"

Emery raises his eyebrows at Theodore and nods. "To my parents' place, Ferdi. Thank you," he instructs his driver.

"Yes, Ferdi. To the Williams's estate! Thank you so much!" Theodore says, mocking Emery's nonchalance.

Emery shakes his head at Theodore, embarrassed by his tone. The beers are kicking in, and Emery is feeling the buzz.

"How come you haven't gotten your own place?" Theodore asks.

Emery leans his head back on the headrest. "Because I travel far too much, and I don't see a point in having my own place at the moment . . ." he says, pausing for a second. "Or maybe I've just never really thought about it, now that you bring it up."

They soon arrive at the Williams's estate. Ferdi pulls up to the gates and types in the code. Theodore sits up and looks out the window.

"I forget just how magnificent this place is!" he says.

As the gates open up, Theodore admires the nicely lit gravel driveway lined with large trees. Every aspect of the landscape is immaculately groomed. Ferdi pulls up to the roundabout by the front door.

Emery steps out of the car and thanks Ferdi before proceeding inside.

As soon as they enter the home, Theodore's eyes widen. He stares at the grand staircases before him.

"I swear, man, every time! Every time I come in here, to this place you call home, it just takes my breath away. It's as if I'm seeing it for the first time," Theodore says in awe.

Before Emery can say anything, Mrs. Williams walks in.

"Boys!" she says, running over to greet them. "Theodore! So lovely to see you, love! It's been too long."

Theodore gives Mrs. Williams a big hug. "It's nice to see you too! It has been way too long. I am getting married soon. I figured I'd invite you all personally, since I am over here hanging out with Emery," he says to her warmly.

Mrs. Williams smiles from ear to ear. "I heard rumors that you were!" she says, teasing. "But we did receive our invitations today. Come on in. Sit down with me. I just finished up a reading for a friend—you know, a psychic reading. It was wonderful."

Theodore and Emery exchange glances.

Victoria Williams continues cheerfully, "And I made some cookies. I would love for you two to join me—unless you want to do your own thing and catch up."

Emery asks Theodore what he wants to do.

"I would love that," Theodore says. "In fact, I was hoping, since you brought up that you just finished a reading, that maybe you would want to do a reading for me?"

"Of course! Come! Sit down!" Mrs. Williams says, delighted.

They all go into the living room and get comfortable by the fireplace. Mrs. Williams sits in her favorite mauve velvet wingback chair and meditates for a second before proceeding.

Emery sits a little farther away on the couch and gives them space.

"Some stuff that comes through is quite personal, dear," Mrs. Williams says. "Do you mind if Emery stays here during the reading?" She patiently looks Theodore in the eyes, awaiting his answer.

Theodore and Emery again exchange glances.

"It's up to you," Emery says to him.

"Umm . . . how personal are we talking?" Theodore asks.

"Very. I don't control what comes up. Sometimes it's very deep personal stuff that no one knows. That is why I am forewarning you." Mrs. Williams raises her eyebrows as she fixes her reading glasses.

Awkwardly, Theodore signals for Emery to leave the room.

Downstairs, Mrs. Williams asks Theodore for his birth date and asks him to say his full name three times.

Theodore takes a seat in front of Mrs. Williams and says his name three times, as instructed. He stares at her intently, and his palms begin to get clammy as he anxiously anticipates what might come up. He can only hope that the reading is positive. Mrs. Williams closes her eyes and begins to focus on, as she calls it, the energy and information that surfaces.

Suddenly, a peaceful smile comes over her face. She opens her eyes and looks at Theodore.

"The young woman you are marrying, Samantha, she is your soulmate. You two have been together before in another life, and you have come back into this physical realm to live your love out in peace. In another life, that love wasn't peaceful, and neither of you could truly be happy—at least as happy as you could've been," she says.

Theodore's eyes widen. "What—" he begins before Mrs. Williams cuts him off.

"You two were supposed to have a child together, but it didn't happen in that incarnation. You might've felt a feeling of familiarity between you two when you first met?"

"Yes, I actually said that to her when we first started to get to know each other. A lot of people thought we moved quick in our relationship when I asked her to move in with me after only three months of knowing her," Theodore says, astounded.

Mrs. Williams nods. "She will be pregnant in no time after you two are married. The child being born to you two is Heaven sent. The child will do life-changing things . . . great things!" she says, but she does not elaborate further on the matter.

She goes on for about thirty minutes more on other things that she feels are vital for Theodore to know. Theodore is astounded at everything he is hearing from his reading. He can't wait to tell his fiancée, Sam, who loves these sorts of things.

Mrs. Williams is still reading Theodore, though she realizes the information coming in is different now. She begins to be flooded with strong visions pertaining to both Theodore and Emery, in relation to the invitation Theodore extended to Emery about the job they would be working on soon. Victoria keeps her eyes closed, doing her best to focus on Theodore, but the information flooding in is too much for her; her brow furrows as she struggles to decipher something. She is curious as to why Spirit is showing her this particular piece of information.

She asks for clarification in her mind so that Theodore won't hear. Spirit shows her a vision over and over of Emery picking up a portrait miniature of someone at the work site. It is of great importance, she realizes, otherwise Spirit would not have shown her. But she is still puzzled by this and doesn't know what to make of it. Spirit doesn't tell her much more.

She looks at Theodore and says to him, "Well, I'm not getting any clarification on what I saw. So I will let it play out for now. Maybe later I can get a clear explanation on it. So sorry, dear."

"That's all right! No worries. You told me enough," Theodore says with a smile.

Emery walks over. "Are you all done in here?" he asks both of them.

"Ah! Yes!" Mrs. Williams says, standing up to give Emery a hug. As she does that, another vision comes rushing in. It startles her for a moment.

"Are you all right?" Emery asks, concerned.

It takes her a second to reply as she continues receiving the vision. "Oh, umm, yes!" she says, leaving it at that.

But what Victoria doesn't say is what she has just seen. Spirit showed her a vision of Emery holding the old portrait in his hand, further emphasizing its importance. Victoria learned that her son is about to once again meet the great love of his life—that fate is gifting him a second chance to get it right. Emery must learn from the mistakes he made in the past. She knows it is time. The premonition Victoria had when Emery was just a baby is about to unfold. That is why Spirit was showing her so much, forewarning her that there is no stopping this.

But Victoria knows it will be incredibly complicated, because his soulmate in question is married at the present moment. The pattern in which things unfolded is repeating itself, except Spirit tells her it has flipped this time. Emery will be tested. His love and desire for his soulmate will be uncontrollable, and—she senses—he will stop at nothing to be with her again.

Victoria is instructed to withhold what she has seen. Emery's desires and darkness will be pulled out of him, challenging who he thinks he is. An old wound will be brought to the surface, a wound he did not know he was carrying around in his soul.

Emery would never imagine that meeting his soulmate, his destined partner, would come with a catch. Victoria gazes at Emery with a tinge of heartbreak in her eyes. The road before him will not be easy, but it is a road he must travel, and travel alone.

"How was the reading?" Emery asks Theodore.

"Good! Very good! She told me Sam and I are soulmates, that we were together before in another life. Isn't it incredible?" Theodore says excitedly.

Emery stares at Theodore with raised eyebrows. "Wow! Really?" he says, smiling.

Theodore nods and sits next to Emery on the leather couch. Mrs. Williams excuses herself and heads to bed.

"Thanks again, Mrs. Williams!" Theodore says to her as she walks out the door and up the stairs.

She gives him a little wave and says, "It's no problem. Good luck to you and Sam. Be good to each other. Good night!"

Theodore and Emery stay up talking until five in the morning.

"So, when is this work thing again?" Emery asks. "This thing you want me to come to with you?"

Theodore laughs, sounding tired and delirious from staying up so late. "It's tomorrow! Wait, tonight? No, tomorrow!" he says through laughter.

"Are you serious right now?" Emery asks, shocked by the suddenness of the proposition. "Man, we should have been in bed hours ago! I am going to be too exhausted to go!"

"Oh, come on, man! Don't act like you don't stay up late already. You'll be fine," Theodore says, reassuring him. "Drink tons of coffee! If you don't mind, I think I'll stay here. We can take off from here and head out at noon."

Emery rolls his eyes. "You're making sure I don't get out of it, aren't you?" he asks, annoyed.

"You know it!" Theodore shouts. "You're hard to get ahold of. Can't let you slip away!"

"Shhh! Shut up! There are people asleep," Emery says, smiling.

"All right, let's go to sleep." Theodore gets up from the couch.

Emery leads the way and takes Theodore to the guest bedroom across from his. They both finally go to bed and wake up within three hours.

Emery wakes up before Theodore and knocks on his door obnoxiously loudly on purpose, as payback for last night.

"Come on! Get up! Wake up!" Emery shouts.

Nannie comes up the stairs, alarmed. "Master Em? What is going on? Why the loud knocking? Didn't your mother teach you to let guests sleep?" she barks.

"Oh, not this one, Nannie. He's an exception," he says with a devilish smile.

She rolls her eyes and heads back downstairs. "Brunch is ready. Hurry down and don't be too long," she shouts on her way down.

"Yup! Thank you, Nannie!" Emery shouts back. Theodore finally opens the door. To Emery's surprise, he is fully dressed and ready to go.

Emery leans in to smell Theodore. "Mmm . . . you showered?!" he says, teasing.

"No, duh!" he says, "Come on, let's go! Don't want to be late."

Emery rushes into his room and gets dressed quickly. He packs his bag with his essentials, and both Theodore and Emery rush down the stairs.

Emery grabs two croissants for the drive.

"Where are you off to in such a rush?" Mrs. Williams asks.

"Work!" Emery says quickly. He gives her a kiss on the cheek and runs to the door.

"Wait! Do you need Ferdi to drive you?" she shouts from the kitchen.

"No, Mother. I will drive us there. Thank you! See you later," Emery shouts as he heads out the door and rushes into the garage, where Theodore is waiting.

"The question is"—Theodore points to the two cars beside him—"the Aston Martin or the Audi?" He rests his chin on his hand playfully, as if pondering which car to take.

"Those are a bit too flashy for this sort of thing. Come on, let's take the Rolls Royce," Emery banters back with a grin.

Theodore smirks. "I love the way you think!"

They speed off to the site and get there within twenty minutes.

"We are so lucky we didn't get pulled over," Theodore points out. "I saw about two cops on the way here."

Emery pulls up to an abandoned estate. "Is this it?" he asks, ignoring what Theodore said.

"Yes, this is it." Theodore looks around for the rest of the crew. He spots them past the gate. "There! Pull all the way in," he instructs Emery.

Emery carefully goes into the property. "I better not leave here with a damn nail or anything of the sort in one of my tires!" he says, rolling his eyes at the thought of having to get it repaired.

"Nothing is going to happen to your tires. Relax," Theodore says while getting out of the car. "Hello, gents!" he shouts out to the others with a smile. "Thank you for coming . . . to my bachelor party!"

Emery frowns, utterly confused. "Bachelor party? You are joking, right?" he asks in disbelief.

Theodore walks toward his other friends without answering Emery.

Emery doesn't quite know what is going on but follows anyway.

They get inside the old, abandoned estate, and everyone starts looking around the place. Emery doesn't know what they're looking for. Perhaps anything of value that they can find?

"Why are we here again?" Emery asks Theodore, still confused by what is going on.

"We are just hanging out and looking around to see what we can find," Theodore says, rummaging through what was once the living room.

"What is the point of this?" Emery presses. The place feels slightly creepy, and he doesn't want to waste his whole day here on a bunch of creepy nonsense.

Theodore sighs. "If you must know, I was hired by some million-aire doctor over in the United States to look for a ring—you know, a piece of jewelry—that could be somewhere here in this abandoned estate. Or, so he says, in any of a number of other abandoned estates around England."

"So, it *is* a job," Emery asks, "and not your bachelor party?"

"Yes! Jesus!" Theodore says, finally having enough of Emery's questions.

Emery puts his hands up. "All right! I just want to know what is going on here! You're being a little too mysterious, and this place is a little creepy."

Alone, Emery heads up the grand staircase and makes his way to what appears to be the master bedroom of the home. He looks through everything, and one item in particular catches his attention. In an old drawer, he finds a small box. Emery pulls it out and dusts it off. He opens it slowly, and inside he finds a portrait miniature of a young woman. She looks to be in her mid- to late twenties, and the portrait seems to have been made sometime in the eighteenth century.

He stares at it and can't help but feel enchanted by the woman in the portrait, as if he has seen her before in a distant dream of some kind. Puzzled and intrigued, he decides to keep it—surely it can't be of any importance to Theodore and his ring-finding mission. He puts the old portrait in his wallet.

He continues looking through the box and finds a handkerchief with the initials E. J. But there is something else. The box also contains an old gun from what seems to be that same era.

Emery heads downstairs and shows the box to Theodore.

"Is there a fat rock in there?" Theodore asks. "On a circle of gold?"

"No, just a handkerchief and an old gun. If you have no interest in it, I'd like to keep it," Emery says, leaving out that he hasn't fully looked through the entire box.

"Sure, be my guest. You can keep it," Theodore says, clearly uninterested.

"What rock are you looking for?" Emery asks.

Theodore admires an old painting on the wall. The painting is falling apart, but it's still possible to make out that it's a woman holding a pristine white rose. On her ring finger she wears a magnificent emerald ring set on a dainty gold band. The rest of the painting needs to be cleaned and restored to be seen more clearly.

"The rock in question is a fat diamond. Or maybe it's an emerald. *That* emerald," he says, pointing to the ring in the painting. "It is said to be almost like a myth. Some people say it exists; others say it doesn't. Some say that woman was buried with it. My job is to search for it. And when I find it, I get shy of thirty million dollars," Theodore says, still admiring the painting in front of him.

"Thirty million dollars?" Emery asks, making sure he heard him correctly.

"Yes, my dear friend. Thirty million dollars. You heard right."

Emery raises his eyebrows and looks at one of Theodore's colleagues. "I'm guessing you're in on this too?" he asks the guy.

The man nods and walks off to look around some more.

"All right, I don't know if we are going to find anything here," Theodore finally says. "The last place she resided was somewhere in this area. They had multiple homes. Maybe it's just nearby."

"Who?" Emery asks.

"This wealthy family back in the eighteenth century, the James family. The story goes that Mr. James gave his wife a fat wedding ring—diamonds or emeralds or something. If it's worth this much now, imagine what it was worth in their time," Theodore says.

Emery looks at Theodore, a bit shocked. "Since when do you take these kinds of jobs?"

Theodore turns to look at Emery, his teal-blue eyes throwing daggers at his friend. "Since the money became too good to say no? Not everyone automatically inherits their billions. Did you forget that? Besides, it's also fascinating to look for this diamond—or emerald—and to dig into the family, even if just for the sake of discovering things. . . . Isn't this why we chose the career of archaeology, anyway?"

"Yeah, I get it! I get it! Relax," Emery says. "I can't help but feel that you're cheapening this career and job by taking anyone's money to find some stupid diamond. Sorry, just my opinion. We are supposed to be looking for *real* artifacts. Like from Egypt! Rome! Fossils in different parts of the world!"

"Emery!" Theodore snaps. "I understand! You're a *purist*. That is your choice, not mine. If I find this thing, then great. Easy money. That is *my* choice. If you don't want to help me, then leave."

"Fine," Emery says, giving up trying to reason with his old friend. "I guess I'll see you around."

Still holding the box he found, Emery heads to his car and drives off. He sees Theodore watching him leave, clearly disappointed, clearly hoping to have Emery's help and support on this job.

On the drive back, Emery can't stop thinking of the woman in the portrait miniature. His curiosity only grows as time passes. He pulls over quickly to the side of the road, takes his wallet out of his pocket, and removes the portrait to look at the woman once more. Something about her eyes is so familiar. Her face, he feels, he has seen before. Emery is sure of it. He decides to take the portrait to his mother and see if maybe she can find out who this woman is.

Emery races back home. He pulls into the driveway and gets out of his car in haste, leaving the door open.

"Emery?" Mrs. Williams comes outside with a concerned look on her face.

"Mother! I need your help with something."

Chapter 4

"What is it, Emery?" Mrs. Williams asks. "I saw you come into the driveway so fast."

Emery pulls out the portrait of the woman and shows it to his mother without letting her finish her sentence.

A stunned look comes over her face. She stares at the portrait and then back at Emery.

"Where did you find this?" she asks, struggling to keep her composure.

"I found it while at this old, abandoned estate with Theodore. This woman's face haunts me. I feel like I know her. But I don't," Emery says in confusion.

Mrs. Williams knows exactly who this woman is; she's seen her before too. Victoria has been having premonitions about Emery's fate in this life from the moment he was born. She has been advised by his spirit guides not to disclose anything prematurely. Emery was born into this incarnation with his own blueprint to follow and fulfill. She can guide and direct him a little bit, but some journeys must be taken alone as we figure out for ourselves the answers we seek. The guides don't want Emery relying too much on his mother for answers. He must go within, follow his intuition and figure things out as he goes. It is part of his fate and destined path.

Victoria struggles to find out what to tell him without divulging too much. Here is what she does know: that the woman in the portrait is his soulmate and destined partner, that the woman has incarnated again in this lifetime. They have karma to work out together, karma that was created in the eighteenth century and is being brought forward into the current one. The woman was his wife in the eighteenth century.

But how can she tell her son this? How can she explain that this important aspect of his past life is coming full circle? Would he even believe her?

"Let's go inside. Come on . . . follow me to the library." She takes hold of Emery's arm.

Emery follows her quickly. He tells his mother he hopes she can answer his burning question of why this woman pulls such an emotional reaction out of him.

They sit down across from each other on couches in the living room. Mrs. Williams takes the portrait miniature from Emery and studies it. She holds it in her hand, focusing on the energy. She closes her eyes, and the information starts flooding in. Mrs. Williams hears Emery's spirit guides as well as her own. She is able to see glimpses of the woman back when the portrait was made; she can discern the woman's emotions, her thoughts, and what she went through. In the midst of the visions that the guides show her, Victoria recognizes Emery's soul and nods in acknowledgment.

"Don't reveal too much at this time," the spirits say to Victoria. "Let things unfold the way they should. This woman means a great deal to his soul. He must find her again and resolve the karma they have together. She was his wife in another incarnation. He loved her so deeply and intensely that his love for her has been carried over into this life." The spirits' voices speak as one, and the power and energy course through Victoria's bones.

Emery waits eagerly for her to say something. He leans forward on the couch and asks, "What is it? Has anything come up?" His blue eyes intently watch his mother.

"Hold on," she whispers.

Her eyes are still closed as she receives the full story about Emery and the woman in another life. She quickly takes the pen and paper in front of her on the coffee table, writing down what she is allowed to reveal to Emery. Mrs. Williams keeps the rest to herself. She knows Emery will find out who he really is eventually. But that is his journey to take. It's his mission to figure it out as he discovers things on his own; she can elaborate on what he finds out along the way.

Mrs. Williams finally opens her eyes and finishes receiving information. Emery's eyes widen.

"She was your wife in another life, Emery."

"Is that why I feel drawn to her?" he asks in disbelief.

"Yes, there is much more to the story. But I can't reveal much to you now, by direct order of not only my spirit guides but yours too."

Emery looks at his mother, appearing unable to really understand what is happening. "This is fate, isn't it? It's no coincidence that I was invited to this place by Theodore. He was an instrument of fate, wasn't he?"

Mrs. Williams simply nods in agreement.

"Did they tell you what I am supposed to do? In this life? Why I came back?" he presses.

"Yes, they told me everything. But some things are yet to be revealed."

"Mother! Please tell me!" he begs, getting down on one knee.

Mrs. Williams shakes her head adamantly. "Emery, I cannot. I would be a fool to not listen to the guides. They know best. They know better than anyone."

"All right then. I guess you could say fate sure has my full attention now." He smiles, but it is clear to his mother that his restlessness is almost unbearable. "But can you answer me this? Will I find her again? Is she here? Reincarnated in this life?"

Mrs. Williams looks at her son's pleading blue eyes and replies with affection. "Yes. You will find her again, but I must let you do that on your own. Follow your intuition; let the universe be your guide. The path for you two to come together again may not be easy. She may resist it at first. Understandably so, with so much personally at stake for *her*. You must be understanding and patient, Emery." Victoria rests her hand softly on Emery's shoulder.

Emery nods. "All right. I will follow your guidance and that of the universe as best I can."

"I know you will. You have been gifted with incredible intuition. Almost as good as mine!" Victoria says teasingly.

They stay and chat in the library for a couple of hours, going over what Spirit told her—that is, only what is meant to be revealed, which isn't as much as Emery wants. Emery shows her the box he found that day at the old mansion with Theodore. Mrs. Williams's eyes light up when she sees the gun. Slowly, she draws it out of the box and then stares at it for several moments.

The thrill of holding an actual tangible item that belonged to Emery in another life makes her tremble slightly. Imagine—her son as someone else! Her eyes inspect every little detail of the gun. Incredible! That a single little object can hold so much karma and history within it seems impossible.

"Emery, this was *yours*. In that other life. These are *your* belongings," she says, her gaze still glued to the gun, inspecting it intently.

Emery stares at her, apparently unsure of what to make of the information.

"I have to tell you, Mother," Emery says. "There is this family that Theodore is looking into. He was hired to find a diamond for some rich multimillionaire doctor in the US."

He pauses for a moment while looking down at the box.

"And?" Mrs. Williams probes.

"And if that's where I found it, does that mean . . . that the diamond in question that Theodore is looking for was in fact *mine?*"

He stops himself, but Victoria can see he wants to ask more. She waits.

"Mother, I think there's a way to learn about my past, about who I used to be."

"Go on," she says. She sets the gun back in its box.

"I've been reading this book about people who explore these things using something called past-life regressions. Have you heard of them?"

"Go on," she says again.

"Well, I was thinking—what if I did something like that? What if I tried to undergo a past-life regression? Maybe I could recover lost memories from the past."

Of course, Victoria knows about this method of trying to uncover the past. Sometimes it works. But other times, things can become confusing. "Maybe," she says quietly to herself.

She knows the past will repeat itself, but in a different way. Some things will occur once more, while other things will need to be amended and changed. Emery is about to discover that what he did in another life caused him so much pain and anguish. Mrs. Williams isn't too sure if Emery will want to relive that again. But she knows all too well that he must to fully understand what he did. For him to completely understand the past, he must relive it and see everything.

"I can conduct the past-life regressions on you myself," she says to him. "I will document everything, much like a research project."

"All right, when do we start?" Emery asks eagerly.

"Tomorrow," Mrs. Williams says, getting up from her seat.

Mrs. Williams has a dream that night. It is of a young woman she believes to be the same one in the portrait Emery has in his possession, only it is in modern times. In the dream, she sees the young woman sitting on the beach and looking out to the ocean on a foggy and overcast day. She taps into the woman's energy, which is happy but with a sense that something is coming toward her beyond her control. Mrs. Williams is able to sense the young woman's fear.

She awakes the following morning with a start.

Mrs. Williams decides to keep the dream to herself, knowing that the spirits have revealed that to her for a good reason. She is eager to get started on Emery's first past-life regression. The spirit guides' message is clear: She will play a pivotal role in Emery's spiritual journey. Her knowledge of the unseen, as well as his fate, will help guide him in the right direction. One thing is for certain—Mrs. Williams knows that the young woman in question is married.

As she pieces everything together, the picture becomes clearer. The young woman's fear and the tough times ahead for Emery have to do with the fact that a choice is going to have to be made. A very tough choice with a lot at stake.

The spirits tell Mrs. Williams the same thing again and again: "Let things happen on their own divine timing. Do not force anything, and do not rush anything. What will be will always be. No one's free will should be violated. The choice must come from her and only her."

Emery and his mother run into each other in the kitchen instead of at the breakfast table. Both decide to have breakfast in the library instead. It is far more private and serene. Victoria wants Emery to be able to stay calm and relaxed. The library also happens to have an extremely cozy atmosphere. Out of all the places in the home, it is the best suited for hypnosis. That's what she wants Emery to agree to.

Emery and his mother walk into the library and settle in, eating and talking briefly about what there is to expect, if anything. She lets him know that some people don't regress at all, because their analytical mind blocks them from being able to do so.

Emery is excited but says he has no expectations; he won't be too bummed out if he doesn't regress on the first go.

They pick a comfortable spot to start.

"All right, Emery. Lie down on the couch over there and get comfortable. I need you to relax and let my voice be your guide." She grabs her pen and notepad as she sits down in the brown tufted leather chair. "I am also going to record this," she adds, bringing the camera closer to her chair.

Emery quickly follows instructions. "No one is going to interrupt the session, right?" he asks as he lies down. He places the soft ivory cashmere pillow behind his head and begins to relax.

"No one will. I let your father know we were going to use this room for about an hour or two. Besides, I locked the door," she says, reassuring him.

"All right."

Emery then begins to close his eyes.

Mrs. Williams starts the pendulum.

"Follow my voice and let it be your guide. Imagine yourself walking on the beach along the water. Focus on the sun as it sets. I am going to regress you back to when you were only a child, at your fifth birthday," she says calmly.

Emery's eyes flutter for a moment and then stop. A smile comes over his face as he sees the day of his fifth birthday, the memories playing before him like a movie. His heart is filled with happiness and a childlike wonder as he relives that moment in his life.

His mother's voice comes in and out softly. "Now I will regress you back to when you were in my womb."

Emery's face becomes peaceful, he can see the lights of the room through his mother's womb. He can hear the piano; Emery recognizes the song she is playing. It is the one she wrote for him. He can hear his father's voice; it is so peaceful and relaxing to him.

His mother's voice comes in again. "Now I will regress you a little further back, to a previous life. Tell me what you see."

She pauses for a moment, waiting for Emery's consciousness to travel to that time in the past.

"I am a man in my late twenties, it looks like. I look about the same as I do now. Same features and everything. The woman in the portrait . . ." He pauses for a moment.

"Yes?" his mother asks curiously. "Who is she? Can you give me her name?"

"Her name is Helena James, and she is my wife," Emery says in almost a whisper. "This is in the eighteenth century, here in England. She is Spanish. She was sent away to live with us because she was disowned by her family for something she did. . . . She was being punished."

Mrs. Williams writes down the woman's name quickly, her blue eyes wide and filled with intense intrigue. They now have her name.

"Do you know what she did? Do you know why she was being punished?" she asks Emery.

"She had an affair with someone her father disliked; he was not of her same class. Her father was very upset, and he separated them. He sent her away to live with us. Her father was a good friend of my father's. They had done business and trade together."

As Emery relays this information to his mother, she listens carefully not only to him but to the guides.

"What is being shown to him is divinely guided," the spirits tell her. "Only the most significant moments of that life—those that we deem worthy of him to know—we will show. Trust that what is being relayed to him is of importance to the journey."

Mrs. Williams writes down what the guides tell her in between what Emery is also saying to her. She doesn't want to leave out any detail that she is able to tell Emery about.

An hour goes by with Emery still in his regression.

He begins to quietly sob.

Mrs. Williams sits up, concerned. "Emery?" she asks, "are you okay?"

Emery whispers in between tears. "I killed him. I killed him because of her. . . . I couldn't take the pain. I couldn't take the betrayal. I wanted him *gone*."

Mrs. Williams listens carefully as she continues to watch him. Emery is in intense emotional pain, almost unbearable for him to remember.

She decides to bring Emery back.

"I am going to bring you back to this moment in time . . . in five, four, three, two, one," she says calmly.

She gives him a couple of moments to recover from the session.

"Go ahead and stay lying down. Do you remember what you saw?" she asks curiously.

Emery opens his eyes slowly, wiping away the tears. "I think so?" he says, unsure. "But it feels like my subconscious or higher self was taking over and that I took a back seat while someone else was driving. It was definitely a strange sensation."

She nods and asks about the tears. "Why were you so upset? You mentioned something about you having to kill someone because of Helena?"

Emery tries to remember what he saw. Heartbreak fills his saddened blue gaze as feelings of shame and anger surface. He is ashamed of his actions—unable to recognize himself in the man he saw.

"Uh, yes. . . . From what I saw, I killed a man named Pierre Martin. I felt so angry and so sad. The emotional pain was unbearable. I loved Helena so much. But she was unfaithful," he says, still lying down on the couch and staring at the ceiling.

Mrs. Williams writes it all down in her notes and shuts the camera off. "Okay, I think we're good for today," she says, excited by what just happened. "This is good stuff!"

Emery gets up slowly and looks at his mother. "Is being exhausted a normal side effect?" he asks.

Mrs. Williams frowns as she thinks for a moment. "You know . . . not that I know of. I guess it could be possible. It depends on how emotionally taxing it is on the person." She shrugs. "Every case is different. Do you need a day to rest or something?"

Emery shakes his head as he yawns. "I don't think so, but I will let you know if anything changes."

Emery gets up from the couch and goes to his room immediately. He lies down on the bed and ends up sleeping for the rest of the day. As he sleeps, he dreams of the home where he and his parents lived in his previous life. He thinks they're dreams, but he's not sure. Perhaps they are memories of his old life.

He sees that his father in that life was also his father in this current life, but he looked different. He had a gray beard and gray hair, with blue eyes and a chiseled nose. Emery dreams of Helena. He recalls his feelings for her, as well as how they met; it was an intense and passionate love. The kind of love he's always dreamed of having in this incarnation.

The following morning, there is a loud and fast knock at his bedroom door.

He turns in his bed as he rubs his eyes, the knocking abruptly waking him from his sleep.

"What?" he says with a tired groan.

The door opens. He turns to look with one eye open, still struggling to see from the drowsiness.

It's his mother.

"Emery, are you all right?" Mrs. Williams asks, extremely concerned.

"Yes. Why?" he asks in a cranky tone.

"After the session yesterday you ran up here and didn't come out at all, not even for lunch or dinner," she says.

"Mother, I am just tired, is all. Nothing to worry about. I haven't even been asleep for that long," he says, annoyed by her overreaction.

"Emery, you slept the entire day right after the session. How am I not supposed to be concerned? We will not have a session today," she says, closing the door behind her.

Emery, still emotionally exhausted, does not mind skipping a session. He rolls over in his bed and goes back to sleep.

Chapter 5

An hour later there is another knock at the door. Emery, at the edge of sleep, can hear the knob turn slowly and the door open.

"Master Em." It is Nannie. "Master Em," she says again, but Emery is too sleepy to respond. He hears her walk to the door and leave.

Just then, the doorbell rings.

Emery hears Nannie greet a woman at the door. He listens carefully; it sounds like Juliet.

"I came by to see if I could speak to Emery," Juliet says. "By any chance, is he around?"

"He is asleep right now," Nannie says.

"Asleep? At this time of day?"

"I assure you, miss, he is. I am as surprised as you are."

The women talk a bit more. Within a matter of minutes, Emery is downstairs and standing behind Nannie, dressed in gray cashmere sweats and a white tee shirt.

Nannie looks back at him, annoyed.

"Oh! Here you are!" She flashes an embarrassed smile and looks back at Juliet. "I think he likes making me look like a liar."

Emery pats Nannie on the back and stifles a laugh. "Thank you, Nannie. I'll take it from here."

"All right then," Nannie says happily. "Enjoy the day." She walks toward the kitchen.

"Juliet," Emery says, "what are you doing here?"

"Uh . . . I just came by to see if you wanted to go with me to the Natural History Museum. I have a project that I have to do for uni, and I was hoping that maybe you could help me?" she asks nervously.

Emery looks down, exhausted. "Juliet, what are you doing?" he says with a sigh; he knows exactly what she's trying to do.

A pained expression comes over Juliet's face. "Emery, I just thought maybe I'd ask you since you're into all that stuff. You could help me get a good grade on this. Please? It's almost eighty-five percent of my overall grade in this class."

Emery brushes his hand through his dark hair and looks at her warily. "Juliet, this better not be some elaborate hoax to make it seem like we're dating. You've done this before. If we go to this museum, we would have to keep a low profile. Do you have any idea how hard it is for me to do that? It's only a matter of time before someone snaps a photo . . . then it's over." He imagines the circus that could ensue.

"It will be all right! No one will spot you, I promise. It will be fast. Please?"

Seeing that she isn't going to let up, Emery feels bad for her and gives in. "Let me grab my sweater, and I'll be right down." As he says this, he's already regretting his decision to go.

Two minutes later, he's climbing into the car with Juliet.

"To the Natural History Museum," he says to the driver in his deep, velvety voice. "Thank you, Ferdi."

Ferdi nods and starts down the driveway to the main gate.

"This is nice, but I would've driven us," Juliet says.

"No, it's quite all right," Emery says. "I prefer to have Ferdi. He's great at losing the photographers, should there be any."

"I can't help but think of how lucky the woman you end up being with will be," Juliet says quietly.

"Juliet!"

Emery's reaction startles her, causing her to jump in her seat a little.

"Emery . . ." she says cautiously.

Emery gazes at Juliet with annoyance and anger. "Stop! Did you not get what I told you last time we spoke? Stop! This is why we can't be friends. You don't understand boundaries and you don't respect me at all!"

"What are you talking about?" Juliet retorts. "Yes, I do!"

Emery closes his eyes, trying to calm himself.

"Why did you *really* invite me to go with you to this museum? You're telling me you really don't have anyone else who could go with you?" Emery asks, hoping she will just be honest and up front about what she is doing.

"Emery, you know so much about history, and given how we left things the last time we spoke, I wanted to hopefully patch things up."

Juliet seems embarrassed that Ferdi can hear the conversation. Emery presses a small black button on the door, and the partition begins to rise. He glances at Ferdi uncomfortably.

"Sorry, Ferdi," he mutters.

"Quite all right, sir. It is probably best," Ferdi says in an unfailingly polite tone.

"Juliet," Emery begins, "I am not interested in being your friend if you are not going to respect the boundaries I have set between us.

I have already told you that I am not interested in you romantically, yet you keep flirting with me and making advances."

Juliet seems to be holding back tears. "Emery, please don't be upset with me. I am just so in love with you! I don't know what to do. I find it impossible to control my emotions. I am human, after all." She struggles to express her words as the tears begin to stream down her face.

Emery sighs, feeling empathy for her. It was not his intention to hurt her—or anyone, for that matter. He is simply not interested in Juliet in that way. Not knowing what to do, he looks out the window, defeated.

They ride in silence for a few moments. "Juliet, please don't cry," he says softly, looking back at her. "I am allowed to say no. I am allowed to say I am not interested, and I don't deserve to be made to feel bad about it. The way that you are right now . . ." Emery's gaze softens into utter heartbreak for Juliet as she continues to cry.

He wipes her tears away gently.

"Juliet, please don't cry. It's going to be okay. You're going to find someone who will love you so much. The way you deserve to be loved. Believe me. It's just not me," Emery continues in almost a whisper as he holds her, doing his best to comfort her.

They arrive at the museum, and Juliet does her best to pull herself together. Ferdi drops them off, and they head inside quickly before they're seen.

They spend the whole day together. Juliet begins to perk up and settles for having Emery's company.

At the museum, a close friend of Juliet's mother spots Juliet and

Emery. She assumes they're on a date and calls Mrs. Montgomery to gossip and to congratulate her on finally getting what she's wanted for her daughter. However, Mrs. Montgomery did not know about her daughter's affairs and is surprised to hear the news. She asks her friend for a photo of Juliet and Emery as proof of what she is relaying to her. Upon receiving the photo, she quickly calls up a photographer friend, who then makes his way down to the museum and waits for Juliet and Emery to come out.

Juliet and Emery head out the same way they came in. Ferdi is waiting for them, but because word got out, they are met by an ambush of what seems like a million photographers. Emery goes out before Juliet; she is unable to see anything amid all the flashes going off. She takes hold of Emery's hand and grips it tightly, still struggling to see where she is walking. Emery guides her through the photographers, and they get in the car.

Emery is quiet for the rest of the ride back to his parents' home. Juliet looks at him anxiously, obviously uncomfortable. While her eyes are on him, she receives a text from her mother, not realizing that Emery sees the message come in. His suspicions are automatically heightened, and he believes Juliet and her mother set it up to make it look as if they were dating.

Upon arriving at the house, Emery walks Juliet to her car.

"Did everything go as planned?" he asks coldly.

She turns around to look at him. "What—"

"Oh, come on, don't give me that! You set this up so you could trick the press and everyone into thinking that we are dating. Come on, admit it! I have had enough of you. I have tried to be nice. I have tried to let you down gently, and you refuse to get it."

Juliet frowns, looking insulted by Emery's accusations. "Emery, what are you talking about?" she shouts at the top of her lungs.

Emery glares at Juliet intensely. "Do you think I'm stupid? I guess you and your mother just know how to play the game, right? Get off my parents' property!"

Juliet looks at Emery in disbelief. "You are asking me to leave?" she shouts back.

"Yes, I am! Leave," he says again, only this time with such a venomous sting that she gasps as though hurt to the core.

"I know what you are thinking, Emery, but I had nothing to do with this. I swear," Juliet says. "Listen to yourself! You are jumping to conclusions without even asking questions or anything?"

"Your mother is known to leak stuff to the press!" Emery exclaims aggressively.

Juliet slaps Emery across the face as hard as she can.

"How dare you make such accusations!" she says. "How dare you insult my family. What could possibly be her motive in this? You are so full of *yourself*!"

"I'm full of myself? Excuse you, weren't you just throwing yourself at me? Crying at me because I didn't want to be with you? You know damn well who my family is! Who *I* am! Better yet, your *mother* knows it too! She is a social climber!" Emery adds, not backing down. "Everyone knows it but you. Don't play stupid. She only wants you to marry me because she wants to be able to say that she is a part of *my* family! She has superficial and shallow intentions, and you know it, Juliet. Don't play dumb."

Emery is so upset that his emotional intensity is on full display;

his usual cool exterior is melted away by the simmering volcanic emotions that lie buried underneath.

Juliet gets in her car without saying anything. She signals for Emery to move, and he gladly obliges, waving her through.

As she leaves, Emery watches her drive off. He takes a deep breath, doing his best to calm himself before going inside. He knows his mother will most likely have heard the news and may be up waiting for him.

Suddenly, the light at the front door comes on, and he hears the door open. Still standing on the gravel driveway, Emery looks down at his feet.

"Emery?" Mrs. Williams calls out, squinting into the darkness to find him.

"Hello, Mother," Emery says as he steps into the light. He slowly walks to where she stands in the doorway.

Mrs. Williams looks sadly at her son. Without his having to speak a word to her about what just occurred, she says calmly, "I already know, and yes, you're right. Mrs. Montgomery called someone and told them you were there."

Emery nods as his suspicions are proven right.

Mrs. Williams lifts Emery's chin gently to look at his eyes. "But Juliet is innocent. She was sadly simply a pawn in her mother's game."

Emery embraces his mother. He can't help but feel drained from the day. "I just want to go away and escape all this stuff," he whispers to her.

She turns her gaze to her son. "You can't escape who you are, Emery. You have a legacy to continue and grow. You are the only heir to the Williams fortune. Maybe just take a trip somewhere far from here, get away for a bit? It isn't all bad."

Emery nods in agreement and embraces her a little tighter. "What would I do without you? You are my saving grace."

She smiles at him and pushes his hair back affectionately. "I love you so much, my son. Go. Get lost for a little while. You never know what you might find," she says, raising her eyebrows. Her eyes twinkle with mystery.

Emery stands back and inspects his mother's gaze curiously. "What?" he asks.

Mrs. Williams heads inside. She struggles to hide the smirk on her face from Emery.

"What do you know?" Emery asks. "You saw something . . . didn't you? There is something coming my way?"

She walks away from Emery, ignoring his questions. "Let me know where you end up going. I'd like to know."

Emery rolls his eyes at her. "You won't tell me because there is a chance that I might ruin it? Right?" he continues, pressing his mother further.

"Maybe," she responds cryptically.

Emery shakes his head and leaves it at that. He rushes to his room.

He is eager to decide where he wants to go. He remembers the book he was reading about past-life regressions and picks it up from the corner of his bed, flipping it over to look at the author's bio. He remembers the name of the town in California—Carmel-by-the-Sea—and searches for it on his phone. It's on the coast of the Pacific Ocean, on the Monterey Peninsula, a ways south of San Francisco.

Emery's interest grows further, and upon doing research on the author/therapist, he stumbles upon her office address and a schedule of upcoming events. He decides to go to Carmel-by-the-Sea, in hopes of meeting her and speaking with her, even if just for a moment.

Emery makes arrangements to take the family plane, books a room in a nearby hotel, and establishes his itinerary. As he does these things, he gets an overwhelming sense that this is meaningful in some way, but he can't quite explain it. The cute little beach town looks like something out of a storybook, with the stores looking like little cottages, immaculately decorated. The homes in the town, too, look like cottages, as if a princess might emerge from them any minute.

Emery immediately falls in love with the images he sees of the town. He decides to leave a week early for the event. Eager to explore the place, he leaves without telling his mother—or anyone, for that matter—where he is going. He is overtaken by exhilaration and adrenaline; unbeknownst to himself, he is answering fate's whisper. The intoxicating ardor of flames under his feet and a spark in his chest propel him forward.

He has Ferdi drop him off at the airport; Emery doesn't even tell Ferdi where he is going. He walks up to the plane and runs up the steps.

"Hello, Mr. Williams. We hope you enjoy your flight," the flight attendant says with a flirty smile. Emery nods and sweetly smiles back as he takes his seat.

"Thank you," he says to her politely.

She gets to work right away and makes Emery a cappuccino. He takes out his phone and looks over his hotel details once more.

"Here you go, sir," the flight attendant says, handing him his beverage. Emery does his best to not give her the wrong impression by any means and tries to keep conversation with her to a minimum. He looks down at his coffee and takes a sip.

"My name is Sophie, by the way," she says to him. Sophie places her hand gently on Emery's shoulder. He looks up at her with a composed gaze. Sophie's green eyes light up as Emery gazes at her, and she smiles.

"I apologize, I don't mean to pester you, sir. . . . I just hope you don't mind a bit of conversation. Flying makes me anxious."

Emery squints in confusion. "But—"

"I know what you're thinking," she interrupts nervously. "I fly around for a living. I know. But it pays well, and I get to see different places, so I put up with the anxiety."

Emery smiles. "Ah, I see. The opportunities outweigh the fear."

He signals for her to sit in the empty seat in front of him as the plane takes off. Emery puts down his cappuccino and gives Sophie a tender smile as he watches her anxiously grip the armrests on her seat. Every time Emery looks at her, she blushes.

Once they're up in the air and the seatbelt light is turned off, she quickly gets up to arrange Emery's bed. He finishes his coffee and pulls out the book he was reading.

"Is that Catherine Jennings's book?" Sophie asks.

Emery turns back to look at her. "Uh, yes. Yes, it is. Have you read it?"

"I have. Do you think it's real?" she questions Emery.

"Yes, I do. I am a very spiritual person, and I like to keep an open mind. Anything is possible."

He gets up from his seat to lie down on the bed Sophie prepped for him. As he passes her, she blinks as though flustered. Emery glances at Sophie quickly while walking down the narrow aisle in the plane, trying not to get too close, but she gulps silently as his arm inadvertently presses against her.

"Thank you," he says.

Sophie nods, visibly struggling to keep her composure. "Umm . . . yes, no problem. If you need anything else, let me know. We land in about thirteen hours. Good night," she says to him and returns to her station.

Emery lies in his bed and looks up at the ceiling pensively. He reaches into his wallet and stares at the portrait of Helena—his true love, the woman his mother verified was his soulmate. He fantasizes for a moment about her, wondering where she is and what she is dreaming about. He wants the opportunity to meet her and get to know her in this life. Emery closes his eyes and drifts off to sleep.

Back home in England, Emery's mother is sitting beside his father as she receives a vision of Emery. She vividly sees the town and the event he is attending. The spirits whisper to her new information. She thanks them for the insight and ponders it.

"Did you have another vision?" Mr. Williams asks gently, caressing her hair away from her face. Her large blue eyes turn to him.

"Yes, I did, love," she answers, keeping her voice low.

"What about?"

"Emery. The guides are speaking to me about him more than ever. The event they informed me about when I conceived him is near."

"Is it good or bad? I remember you mentioning it to me, but you didn't quite elaborate on any details, love."

She smiles at him without saying anything for a second.

He stares, awaiting her answer patiently. He's always been so in love with her mystique and intuitive aura.

"All in good time," she says simply. As she looks up at the dark night sky, she glimpses the stars. She thinks of Emery and asks that the spirits protect and guide him.

Chapter 6

After a long and restless flight, Emery lands at Monterey airport, right near the vast expanse of the Pacific Ocean. His driver is waiting for him as the plane doors open.

"When will you be departing Carmel?" Sophie, the flight attendant, asks him. She hands him his messenger bag and book.

"I arrived a week early for the event I am going to, but to answer your question, I don't really know. I will play it by ear."

He takes the book from her hand and thanks her once again. She watches him walk to the car as his driver opens the door for him. Emery gets in and waves goodbye to her with a smile.

"Did you have a good flight, sir?" asks his driver as they pull onto the main road.

"I did, thank you. I am Emery Williams," Emery says, introducing himself.

His driver smiles at him through the rear-view mirror. "Nice to meet you, Mr. Williams. I'm Jeremy, and I'll be your driver for the remainder of your trip."

"Nice to meet you, Jeremy! And please, call me Emery."

Jeremy nods and smiles. He takes Emery promptly to his hotel and helps him with his bags. Upon arrival, Emery looks around at the hotel and finds it incredibly charming. The energy of the town is otherworldly. Photographs just don't do it justice.

He goes to his room and settles in, but he is so eager to explore the town that he finds it hard to sit in his room for very long. He reaches for his camera and decides to go for a walk. After wandering for a while, he stumbles upon the downtown area and takes a few photographs. The place is so much more enchanting in person. He grabs some coffee at one of the local coffee shops and makes his way to a realtor's office. As he browses the listings posted on the front window, a petite blonde woman with blue eyes, probably in her mid-forties, pops out of the office to greet him in a peppy voice.

"Hi! Can I help you with anything?" she says to Emery with a big smile across her face.

He glances at her quickly while trying to look at a particular listing that caught his eye—a home off of Scenic Drive.

"Yes, actually. I like this home that you have listed here, and I was wondering if I could see it, by any chance?" Emery flashes his captivating smile, knowing that it won't fail him.

"I would love to!" she says, excited. "I am Marie Jenson. I take it you are not from here?"

Emery smirks slightly. "What makes you say that?" he asks, pretending not to know what gave her that impression.

"I've never seen you around here before. It's a small community, and when you've been here as long as I have, you start to distinguish the familiar faces from the tourists' faces. . . . Oh, and your accent!" she says, laughing.

Emery chuckles. "Oh, yeah, I thought that might have something to do with it."

He steps into her office as they chat about the homes in the area and fill out some forms with his information.

"Have you been here before?" Marie asks him.

Emery looks down at the forms, clipboard and pen in hand. "First time. I'm here for an event. But I came a week early to explore the town. And now I think I may buy a home here. It is insanely beautiful!"

"Oh, that's so nice! I hope you enjoy your time here. It is incredibly beautiful, for sure! My family has been here for four generations," Marie says, and Emery hands her the clipboard and pen with the filled-out forms.

"Thank you." Marie looks them over. "When would you like to see the home that you liked? No one is staying in it right now, so we can head on over if you want."

Emery quickly stands up from his seat. "Right now is a good time! I'm not doing anything else."

Marie grabs the keys for the home out of the lockbox in her desk. "We can walk or we can take my car," she says.

"Either one. I don't mind. I'll let you choose," he says.

"All right! Let's walk. It is not far at all, and we can chat some more."

She leads the way out of the office. They walk all the way down the street and then stop at Scenic Drive, the last street before the beach. Emery is taken aback by the view before him. The sea breeze, the clouds, and the gloomy beach weather enchant him completely.

"This weather reminds me of England," he says to Marie.

"Does it? Well, you'll feel right at home here. I think it's perfect weather. It never gets too hot."

They walk up the steps to the home. Emery looks back at the view of the ocean. He's in love with it already and immediately thinks of having this home as his safe haven, away from the world of chaos in England.

Emery follows Marie through the front door, and they go from room to room together.

"What do you think?" Marie asks him when they're about halfway done.

"Oh, I love it!" Emery says. "I don't think I want to see anything else. This one will do."

Marie grins excitedly. "Really? That much, huh?"

"Yes, it feels right. I think I'll take this one. And to ensure they accept the offer, I'll give them cash at asking price," Emery says calmly.

Marie is stunned and overcome with excitement. "Oh, my god! Okay, I'll get the paperwork started!"

Emery laughs at her little squeals of happiness. "Thank you," he says. He gives her a hug, and they make their way back to the office.

"Is there any chance that I would be able to move in before thirty days?" Emery asks her eagerly.

Marie looks down at her phone and sees an incoming call from another client, but she sends them to voice mail to give Emery her full attention. "I will ask. I don't see why not. They don't reside in this home," she remarks confidently.

Emery feels very good about his decision to move to Carmel-by-the-Sea and the new home he is buying. Marie is so sweet and easy to work with. They become friends rather quickly.

"What are you doing for the rest of the evening?" Marie asks. "I would like to take you to dinner if you don't mind?"

Emery smiles happily. "Uh, sure. I was actually starting to think about what to do for dinner."

"Perfect! I know a place around here. The food is spectacular. It's at a hotel. The Aulberge?" she says.

"What are the odds. That's where I am staying."

"Oh, well, perfect then! The Aulberge it is. I'll meet you in the lobby of the hotel at seven?"

"Yes! I'll see you then. Thank you for everything." Emery shakes her hand and makes his way to the beach.

Everything is within walking distance from where Emery is staying, right in the heart of downtown Carmel-by-the-Sea. He feels right at home. He takes his shoes off as he reaches the sand, which feels soft and pristine under his feet. His blue eyes stare out at the ocean waves crashing on the beach. A peaceful smile comes over his face. He is in Heaven, and no one knows him here. He has finally found a place where he can be at peace, a place where anything can happen.

As he looks out at the horizon, he hears someone call out, "Helena!"

Emery turns to see a golden retriever running toward him.

"Helena!" a woman shouts at the dog.

The dog jumps up on Emery excitedly.

"I am so sorry!" the woman says as she rushes up to him, out of breath. "She loves the beach and just gets so excited!"

Emery smiles as he pets her dog. "It's all right! No worries."

"Nice accent!" she comments, smiling. "I am Dalia, by the way." She extends her hand out to Emery. Her soft, petite hand almost disappears into his.

"Nice to meet you, Dalia. I am Emery. Interesting name for your dog. Helena?" He's struck by the coincidence—this dog and the beloved woman he's here to learn more about. If, that is, all goes well with the book author and therapist, Catherine Jennings, whom he's eager to meet.

"Yeah, I wanted something regal," she says, laughing.

Emery smiles and nods.

"Bye then! Sorry for the intrusion," she says softly as she runs after her dog.

He watches her run off and decides to get back to the hotel.

Was it the universe whispering to him? *Hearing her name can't be a coincidence,* he thinks to himself. His subconscious thoughts have put the law of the universe into motion. One thing is for certain: His heart longs for this woman—Helena—that his heart and soul knows but his mind doesn't. *I must find her,* he thinks to himself.

Right before he enters his hotel room, he gets a message from Marie to confirm their dinner in an hour. He rushes in to freshen up and get dressed.

He notices that he is going about the day as if on autopilot, motion by motion. Helena is consuming his very soul.

He arrives fifteen minutes early to the restaurant, and he notices that it is a very cozy little place. It makes him feel as if he's been transported to a different country, somewhere in a small town in Europe. He spots Marie and walks over to her.

"Hi!" she says, looking happy to see him again. "This place is adorable, isn't it?"

"Hi. Yes, it is. It is incredibly charming," Emery says as he takes his seat.

"I got the paperwork done," Marie says. "The owners were very happy and surprised with your offer. They didn't even let me finish talking before they shouted *yes!*"

Emery raises his eyebrows in astonishment. "That's incredible! I am so happy that it worked out. What did they say about the move-in time frame?"

Marie puts her menu down quickly. "They said you can move in immediately."

"Really? Oh my god, that's great! I'll have to go furniture shopping then!" Emery remarks.

Marie and Emery spend only about an hour and a half at dinner.

This move feels good, and he feels as if it is a step in the right direction. After dinner, Emery stays up late writing poetry. He can't sleep. For the rest of the week, he spends his time moving in and furnishing his new home. He doesn't speak to anyone back in England, not even his beloved mother.

He figures she knows what is going on anyway. *Even if I did keep in contact, it would defeat the purpose of the trip,* he thinks to himself.

Rose

Chapter 7

The waves crash on the shore as I contemplate my life. My toes press into the cool, soft sand of Carmel-by-the-Sea, a seaside town on Northern California's Pacific coast. The sun is kept hidden by the fog, and I barely notice anyone around me. I always find solace in being alone with my thoughts, and I know I need that today. My mind wanders, and I let it. Each time my mind flits off in a new direction, it brings me back a new revelation to ponder. This is good, because I'm on my way to visit Jess, my astrology teacher. We're going to look over my astrological chart today, and she always suggests I take some time to let my mind wander as I prepare for our meeting.

Ever since I was a little girl, I've had an overwhelming need to be free. Free from my family's expectations for me and what I should be, do, and have. It was something I couldn't quite put my finger on at times, but the sensation lingered, haunting my soul every day. I craved personal freedom from my invisible cell. Constant fantasies flooded my dreams—about leaving my hometown and settling else-where, leaving everything and everyone I knew behind and starting over. I wanted to disappear without a trace; only then could I truly be free in the way that I dreamed. I yearned to discover for myself what my beliefs were. I have always had a certain disdain for tradition, mainly because my parents are so traditional: Catholic and by-the-book conservatives.

A large pelican flies by; the gloomy gray sky looks as if it is about to rain any minute. I enjoy the rain very much and feel lucky that Carmel gets so much of it.

There are a lot of people out on the beach today, enjoying the weather with their families and pets. The ocean waves appear almost teal—a deep greenish-blue—as they crash on the shore. A man stands on the rocks nearby, doing his best to photograph the pelican that was previously flying. He must be a photographer, perhaps from the aquarium in Monterey. They come to Carmel a lot, along with marine biologists who swim about as they study the marine life and seaweed close to the shore.

I enjoy coming onto the beach and seeing the little dogs running around gleefully, greeting everyone and anyone who passes them by. I can't go long without feeling the cold, soft sand beneath my feet. It is incredibly grounding. My natural place is by the sea.

I think back to my childhood in Hollister, a small agricultural town about an hour away from here. It was a lovely place to grow up. But living here with my husband feels just perfect. Our home is right by the beach, and I can't imagine myself living in a place like Hollister again—much too far from the ocean. The beach here in Carmel is the one place that feels peaceful, where I go to realign my chakras and de-stress.

As I continue my walk, I think about the ideas I've been mulling over lately, and I worry that my new interest in learning about my past—by which I mean past lives, incarnations, regressions—might not sit well with my husband. I'm not sure what it will mean for our relationship, or what it will mean for me either.

I have always been a very spiritual person. This part of me was just locked away and didn't emerge until I grew up and moved away from my family's influence. As I've grown and evolved as a soul, I have allowed myself to believe in my own unorthodox views. They're unusual compared to what I was taught growing up—so much so that my family might think I'm a nut and lock me up in a looney bin straightaway if I divulge my beliefs to them.

It took my family members by surprise when I introduced them to Phillip—the man I chose to marry—in part because my husband is the complete opposite of me. On top of that, our relationship was one of those whirlwind romances you hear about, where it came out of the blue and the attraction was through the roof. We make no sense as a couple, but the chemistry is undeniable.

In and out of thought, I struggle to ground myself in the sand. I stop and take a deep breath, focusing on the cool sand beneath my feet, bringing me back to the present moment. Something I struggle with is my mind and heart conflicting constantly, driving me insane. All one can do is enjoy the present moment, but I fail every time. I glance over at the pelican, still on the rock before the photographer, as it prepares to fly off. I usually find myself envying the flying birds for how free they seem.

My mind wanders once more, and I think about Phillip and how he's really neither spiritual nor religious. As an orthopedic surgeon, he is extremely analytical. Everything Phillip believes in is based on facts that cannot be denied. He doesn't act on faith very much, unlike me. Some might wonder how our relationship could possibly work, but it just does; we balance each other out—even after five years of marriage. He spends most of his time working; most days he is so swamped that we don't see each other much, despite living under the same roof. Because I am a writer, my job allows me to work from anywhere and allows for flexibility.

I do wish Phillip shared my passion for delving into my past, though. I've been undergoing regressions and progressions with an esteemed psychiatrist, Catherine Jennings, who has been performing them for years on her patients. Many people claim that it has helped them with anxiety, depression, fear of death and the unexplainable, and severe phobias. Catherine has become my good friend and mentor. We met about six months ago through a mutual acquaintance. Jess, my astrology teacher, suggested she would be a great person to see regularly as I began to explore my beliefs and expand my consciousness. We have yet to start on regression therapy, but we have been prepping for that for the last six months.

The next time I see Catherine, I will experience my first session. I must admit I find myself fighting the possibility of past lives being real. Part of me proceeds with caution, not knowing what to think. I am open minded, but when Jess first mentioned it to me through the subject of astrology, I did not know what to make of it. But then I started to ruminate within myself.

What have I got to lose? Maybe this is the moment that I have been waiting for. I should jump into the unknown and explore all I can about this subject. Maybe this is the universe's cosmic nudge to steer me toward my destiny. From what I have learned through astrology, this situation ties in to what I have come here to learn.

I have begun documenting important pieces of information that Jess and Catherine have exposed me to. So far, both have been incredible instruments on this journey. Catherine has taught me to meditate regularly and has instructed me to learn to listen to my intuition—disconnecting from my mind for a bit to let my spirit speak more.

Chapter 8

The following morning after Phillip leaves for work, I wake up and make myself some coffee to drink while I get ready for my appointment with Catherine. The nerves start to set in, but I do my best to ward them off.

I drive up to Catherine's office and sit in my car for a moment, trying to shake off some of my anxiety. I don't really know what to expect or what I will see for sure, but all I can do is trust that whatever I see is what my guides want me to see the most. I take a deep breath and walk up to the front door.

Catherine's office is one of those old Victorian homes that has been converted into a business building. It is very charming and makes you feel as if you have traveled back in time. Little shrub hedges line the walkway to the door, adding curb appeal. I can hear laughter and two women's voices inside.

Before I can knock, the gold doorknob turns, and the door swings open. Behind it, a woman in her late forties or early fifties looks startled to see me. Her appearance is very polished and expensive looking, and I can't help but admire her hair. It is silky smooth and looks as though she got a professional blowout from the hair gods themselves.

"Oh! So sorry. I wasn't expecting someone to be on the other side!" she says with a big smile and a bit of a giggle. I smile back at her and move to the side so she can get by.

"It's all right! I was about to knock. . . . Perfect timing, I guess," I say, somewhat awkwardly.

The woman says goodbye to Catherine, who is standing behind her, and makes her way down the walkway.

"Hello! Are you ready?" Catherine says with a warm smile as she extends her hand out to greet me. Her green eyes light up excitedly.

"Yes, although a little nervous," I confess, doing my best not to let my anxiety show too much.

She smiles and leads the way inside. "Come on in! Have a seat. Get comfortable, because the more comfortable you are, the better and faster you can go deeper into the meditative state and access more memories."

She takes a seat in a leather wingback chair, puts on her reading glasses, and grabs a notepad and pen. "I'm making my own notes to add to your file. You can record your session today if you'd like. Jess told me you are documenting this on your own for your personal records, correct?"

"Yes," I say, getting comfortable on the couch.

"Okay," she says, "let's see what we can uncover today."

I smile and say nothing. My hands are icy cold. They usually get that way when I am extra anxious.

"Do you have any questions for me before we start?" Catherine asks, looking back at me.

"How long are the sessions usually?" I ask quickly.

"Ummm . . ." She pauses for a second. "Two hours, maybe three.

I usually will max out at three, but sometimes the guides have a lot to say or show you. You are my last appointment for today, so we are good on time if the session runs a little longer. But if you want to stop at one hour, we can definitely do so. Just let me know."

"Okay, sounds good."

"Okay, so let's get started. I am going to ask a couple more questions, and then we can begin the regression," Catherine says. She flips open her notebook. "Who is the most significant person in your life? Who do you get along with well? Who do you not get along with well? And lastly, is there anything you would like answered about your life? For example, are there certain blocks you feel in receiving love, expressing love, feeling loved, or anything of that nature?"

I pause for a moment and try to answer the questions in the order that she asked them. "My brother, my husband, and my parents are the most significant in my life. I love them very much, and we have an incredibly strong bond. We can talk about anything and understand one another very easily."

I let her write some of that down before continuing. "It's only my brother and me, and of course, my parents. My extended family is very large, but in regard to siblings, it is only my brother and me."

Catherine writes some more. She looks up at me to ask another question. "And your brother, is he younger or older?"

"Younger. By two years," I say.

"Younger . . . by two . . . years." Catherine repeats it in a whisper as she jots it all down.

"I would say that I am cynical when it comes to romantic love. Don't get me wrong, I love my husband, but I can't help but wonder what the hell it's for. What is the purpose?" I say everything without holding anything back. "The love a mother has for her child, I get that. Wholeheartedly! But romantic love, it just seems like a waste of time. Sorry." I stop myself halfway; I don't want to be over-the-top.

"What do you mean? What about your husband? You say you love him very much, yes? I'm confused. That's what life is about: love. Love is the very reason why we exist. Love is everything. I truly hope I can change your mind, or at the very least expand your mind and heart on the matter." Catherine looks at me with confidence, her soulful green eyes warm. "You're much too young in this life cycle to think that way. But yet, it may have something to do with a past life of yours? Maybe you're carrying those feelings of disappointment from another lifetime."

She pauses for a second and then excitedly says, "Let's find out."

I lie back on the sofa and get comfortable. My head sinks into the down pillow, and I look up at the ceiling, awaiting Catherine's instructions.

"Close your eyes," she begins. Her soft voice helps calm my nerves.

"Relax. Take a deep breath in and a deep breath out. Focus on your breathing. Allow your legs to relax; feel your muscles relaxing. Now your arms, relax those muscles. Release any tension. Good," she says.

I can feel my body relaxing, my limbs feeling heavier and heavier as my mind begins to drift.

"Focus on my voice and let it be your guide. If a scene becomes too intense, you can always float above what is happening and detach."

Within a minute, I enter into deep hypnosis.

"You're always in control and you are safe. Whenever you want to stop, let me know. Now, imagine yourself in a wonderful garden filled with the most magnificent roses. Observe the bees buzzing about, landing ever so gently on some of the roses. Find a nice spot in the grass area to lie down and relax in this serene environment. Still focus on your breathing. Now, allow yourself to go back in time. Go back to a childhood memory."

Catherine pauses for a moment, allowing time for the memory to surface.

"Now," she continues, "I want you to be there in three, two, one. Remember everything in detail. Who is there with you? What are you doing?"

I stay quiet for a second, observing the moment I am seeing,

"It's the first day of kindergarten, and I am five years old. All the mothers are gathered at the door, dropping their children off for their first day. I walk in cautiously with my mother behind me. I can see the cubbies on my right-hand side, and one has my name on it. My mother puts my backpack in it. I walk past the cubbies and see a large carpet. Everyone is already in their spaces around the carpet. The teacher is sitting at the center, and he sees me. I try to bolt back to my mother, but when I turn back, I see that my mother is leaving. My mother rushes through the other mothers and makes it out the door. I try to go after her in a panic, but the group of mothers stand in my way. I begin to scream and cry. The teacher, Mr. Schneider, comes running to grab me and places me with the rest of the class, but I am fighting him. I am amazed at his strength, because he is maybe in his mid- to late sixties. I am kicking and screaming loudly, but I finally calm down and take my seat with the other children."

I relay this to Catherine but notice that I'm having another vision. "I am also seeing another moment. It's the same year, except it's Christmastime. The class is decorating their Santa hats. We are using glitter glue to write our names; the green glitter glue is my favorite. All the colors look so magical to me with the touch of glitter in them. I feel happy. This is the moment I fall in love with the joy of Christmas."

My voice cracks slightly. My eyes begin to water as the joy from that moment in my childhood becomes almost overwhelming.

Catherine listens quietly and lets me stay in the moment for a couple seconds more.

"Okay, good," she says calmly. "Now let's go back further, back to when you were in your mother's womb. Four, three, two, one, be there. Remember everything. What can you see? What do you feel?"

"I can hear women talking. I think it's my aunts on my mother's side. They're talking about a baby shower."

"Whose baby shower? Your mother's?" Catherine asks.

"Yes," I answer.

"Okay, now let's go back even further. To the life before this one. Remembering everything in detail. Four, three, two, one. What do you see? Who is there with you?" Catherine asks.

I suddenly find myself in England, walking toward a grand-looking manor. "I am in England. I think it's sometime in the eighteenth century."

"Okay, and what are you doing there? Who is with you? Do you see anyone?"

"I am walking toward a very grand manor. It looks like a palace. I live here with my husband, Emmett, and two children."

Catherine allows me to see that life in full detail without interrupting much, only asking an occasional question every now and then. Her voice fades in and out ever so softly.

I look down at my feet and see myself wearing a beautiful silk long-sleeve dress; it is springtime. I have long dark hair, almost black. My skin is very fair. My name is Helena, I was born in Spain, and at this point in time, I am twenty years old. The grounds of the estate look magnificent, the landscaping immaculately kept. I walk up the steps, and in the front door, I see my husband, Emmett, playing with our children. A feeling of shame and guilt comes over me, so much so that I can feel it in my chest. It consumes me. I hurt him. I betrayed him. I still carry those feelings within my soul in this lifetime. Tears begin to stream down the sides of my face.

"If the scene becomes too intense, you can disconnect," Catherine says softly.

"I'm okay," I say. "I need to feel this. I needed to remember this."

I begin to be taken further back—back to where this started, before I was sent over to England as punishment by my father for having fallen in love with someone he deemed unworthy. I find myself back in Spain, a little bit younger than before—seventeen, maybe eighteen years old. I loved riding horses; they were a big passion of mine during this time. I am one of the best riders, even better than all my brothers. My eldest brother resents this because I am female and younger than he is, but only by three years.

I can see the boy I fall in love with: Pierre Martin, a young man from France. He is beautiful and bright. I recognize his soul; it is clear he is also my husband in this lifetime. Seeing him again brings back all those old feelings—feelings that time itself could never fade, centuries apart or even worlds apart. The disguise of another flesh could never fool me. I'd recognize his soul and gaze anywhere; his enchanting green eyes watch me tenderly.

And now it all clicks into place as I regain these memories. My father hired Pierre for help around the estate, specifically with the horses and stables. We spend a lot of time together, and my father is beginning to suspect that Pierre has feelings for me. I can see my father watching Pierre and me as we interact and ride around the vast estate together.

On one particular instance, I give my horse to Pierre, and as we ride back in near the stables, my father takes the reins from me and leads the horses in.

"Your mother is asking for you, Helena," he says to me.

"Did she say why?" I ask.

My father stares at me sternly. "Just go."

I glare back at him with an unamused frown.

I always give my father a hard time. We don't get along, and I have quite the talent for disobeying him and doing as I please—rightfully so, because he is a tyrant and obsessed with control, although I don't take it personally. I know that he is like that with everyone. He is fixated on me because I refuse to bow down to him and follow his outrageous orders. Everyone else, for the sake of being left alone, will listen to him and do as he asks; they don't want to ruffle his feathers. He is cruel and has a mean temper, but I don't care. I am much too headstrong to go along with any of his absurdity just to appease him.

He is well known for being quite the snob too. Anyone who isn't from money or high social status certainly has no chance of marrying into his family, let alone marrying his daughter. I know he relishes enforcing his will on anyone he can, but he seems to get a particular kick out of ruining any young man's chances of getting close to me, especially in the romantic sense.

I detest my father, and my father detests Pierre—a man who doesn't meet the social standing my father requires of anyone who comes near me.

As soon as I leave the stables, my father approaches Pierre and asks in an intimidating tone, "Are you enjoying it here, Pierre?"

Pierre's beautiful and innocent face turns to look at my father; he respects him a lot as a man and as his employer. "Yes, sir," he replies politely. "You have a wonderful home here."

"I do. Yes, I do," my father says while admiring the horses, "but nothing quite as wonderful as my daughter—Helena. Wouldn't you agree?"

They both grow quiet, and the tension in the air is uncomfortable. My father stares at Pierre with a stone-cold expression on his face.

Pierre senses my father's disapproval of him as a suitor for me. "She is lovely, and she has a beautiful soul," he says simply.

He continues his chores around the stables, but my father relentlessly stays around, making sure his opinions and objections are heard loud and clear by Pierre.

"I will only tell you this. If you cross the line and get romantically involved with my daughter without my blessing, the very wrath of Hell will come down upon you. I am not someone you want as an enemy, so do yourself a favor and keep away from her. For your health and well-being."

Pierre nods and says nothing.

My father makes his way out of the stables. "Good job with the horses!" he says, smirking. Then he stops in his tracks. "Oh, and do wash up. You're invited to dinner with us."

Pierre's heart is racing; it is far too late for the warning. He has fallen in love with me and I with him. What started in that lifetime is something that will come to last multiple lifetimes. We just didn't know it then.

Pierre washes up for dinner and puts on his best attire. He looks very handsome. His chiseled jawline and strong body make the clothes look incredible. He walks into the grand entryway and waits in the living room by the fireplace. My brothers—Emmanuel, Daniel, and Ricardo—all come running in, loud and rambunctious.

"Good to see you! It's about time my father invited you," Daniel says. He is the sweetest of the bunch. I recognize him as my brother in my current lifetime. We are very close. He is also one of my soulmates, I am told, but I already knew that. We understand each other eerily well.

"Thank you," Pierre says politely. He is a little uneasy, keeping to himself what my father told him earlier.

My mother walks in, elegantly dressed. "Dinner is served!" she says. "Come on, Pierre. You can sit next to me."

Pierre gets up from the couch and takes my mother's hand, and right at that moment, he sees me coming down the stairs. His eyes cannot hide what he feels. My mother looks at Pierre and simply smiles.

"Pierre! I didn't know you were joining us tonight!" I say excitedly.

Pierre walks over to the end of the steps and reaches out to take my hand. "Yes, your father invited me," he says, his heart racing.

"Speaking of your father, here he is now," my mother says.

My father walks in—immaculately dressed, as always. He sees Pierre standing next to me and glares at him. My mother takes notice, and an unamused expression comes over her face. While not surprised, she is irritated at how rude my father is being.

"Let's eat, shall we? All this glaring is making me hungry," my mother says, mocking my father in a way only she can.

I try to contain my laughter but fail. Pierre looks at me, wide-eyed; he is still a little uneasy from the exchange of looks between him and my father.

"Come on," I say, "it'll be all right." I take his hand in mine and squeeze it just a little in reassurance.

We walk into the grand dining room and take our seats. Pierre sits right beside me.

"Pierre, you don't want to sit next to me?" my mother asks, a little hurt. My father stares at Pierre and me, still upset.

"He can sit next to *me*," I say quickly back to my mother, completely ignoring my father's stare.

"You two have grown quite close," my mother says, surprised. "Helena doesn't like anyone."

"Must you tell everyone that?" I ask her, annoyed.

"It's true," Daniel says. "She only loves me because I'm her brother, and even then, I had to earn her love."

I stare at Daniel with a raised eyebrow. "Is this dinner going to be centered around me and what I like and don't like?"

"Calm down. There you go," says Ricardo, "always so angry anytime someone points out something you do or how you are."

I roll my eyes at him.

Pierre gazes at me lovingly and smiles a little, but he says nothing.

My father is unusually quiet during dinner and just observes Pierre and me angrily.

"Did you invite him just to make him as uncomfortable as possible? You are being rude to your guest. Show some manners!" I say defiantly to my father.

A mortified look comes over Pierre's face.

"Helena!" my mother shouts in shock.

I don't even give him time to respond. I put my utensils down and grab Pierre's hand.

"Come on, let's go!" I say. We rush out of the house and run over to the stables.

My father rises from the table, and I can hear his shout.

"Helena!" His voice almost echoes throughout the place with an utter rage.

I laugh as I run with Pierre.

"What are we doing?" he asks me, scared. "Your father is going to kill us."

"No, he won't! Come on. Grab a horse. Let's go for a ride," I say, mounting Remy, my beloved black stallion. Pierre mounts Isabella, my mother's beloved mare, and we ride off into the night together.

The night sky is magnificent above us. The stars shine and illuminate the night, and the wind blows through my hair. It makes me feel so alive. I lead the way down to a remote area on the beach that my family hardly frequents. There lies an old shipwreck that I used to visit often as a child, playing make-believe and all sorts of games. I still go there whenever I want to be alone. Pierre and I tie up our horses and head inside. He is surprised to see a bed and some books in there, as well as candles and other things.

"You come here often?" he asks, looking around.

"Yes," I say, signaling for him to make himself comfortable on the bed. "We can spend time here without anyone bothering us."

"What about your father? Surely he must know of this place?" Pierre asks, still worried.

"I think he does, but I don't care," I say, incredibly relaxed about the whole situation.

Pierre doesn't share my feelings. "He warned me today," he confides in me.

I look at him with a confused frown. "About?"

"You . . . and me. The time we spend together. He doesn't like it." Pierre looks down, sadness engulfing his eyes.

"He doesn't like much. It's nothing to be afraid of," I say, unbothered. I lie down on the bed and make myself comfortable.

"I am in love with you, Helena," Pierre blurts out.

We stay still for a moment. I look at Pierre, glad that he feels the same way as me.

His green eyes burn with an unquenchable desire.

I smile softly and make my way closer to him. "I love you too, Pierre."

Pierre kisses me and unleashes a passion of love that neither one of us knows how to control in that moment, and so we don't try. That night we consummate our love without anyone's approval but our own. We don't care what might happen, for we love each other, and nothing can get in the way of that. Not my father or time itself.

We spent that wonderful night together in each other's arms, but it would be our last for a long, long time.

Chapter 9

The following morning at sunrise, Pierre and I are lying in bed together, peaceful and in love. We are awoken by a thunderous sound. It sounds as if a whole armada of horses is galloping toward us. Pierre and I rush to put our clothes on and head outside to see what is going on.

It is my father and some of his henchmen.

Pierre is frightened by what may come next. I stand in front of Pierre as my father walks toward us. The anger and wrath on my father's face make it seem as if Pierre and I just killed his first-born son.

"You blatantly disobeyed me!" my father yells as he strikes me across the face. The blow knocks me down on the sand.

Pierre punches my father in the face as hard as he can and pushes him back. "Don't you dare touch her again!" he yells.

My father grasps Pierre by his neck and pins him on the boat as my father's men draw their swords.

"You disobeyed me! And you will pay a heavy price for it. The both of you." My father lets go of Pierre and leaves him there, and then he violently grabs me by my arm and forces me on the horse.

"You will never see her again!" my father says one last time to Pierre, and we ride off to the estate.

When we arrive, my mother and brothers are out front. My brother Daniel's eyes meet mine, and I can see sadness in them. The staff are loading luggage onto the carriage.

"What is happening?" I frantically ask Daniel.

"I am sending you away," my father says, dragging me toward the carriage. "To England. You are not welcome here any longer. You disobeyed me, and this is the price for that!"

I begin to cry and scream as I try to hug Daniel. "You can't do this!"

"I can and I will! Say your goodbyes to your mother and brothers, for you will never see them again!" my father yells mercilessly.

I try to plead with my mother, but she is far too submissive in this moment to do anything. She kisses me goodbye as tears stream down her face, and then she quickly heads inside. I watch her leave; it is the last time I will see her in this lifetime.

The emotions wash over me, and I am engulfed in them.

One of my father's men ties my hands and forces me into the carriage.

"Father, please! You can't do this!" I scream out at him.

He grabs my hands while they are tightly bound and coldly looks into my eyes. "You're lucky I don't have you hanged for disgracing the family. Imagine if all of Spain found out! How it would impact our family! Consider this mercy!" he says with his teeth clenched.

He angrily signals his men to take me away.

As the horses begin to pull the carriage, I can hear Pierre call out my name, his voice filled with despair.

"Helena!"

I kick the door open and jump out of the carriage to see Pierre behind us. He tries to run toward me as he continues to call out for me.

My father's men grab me and throw me back in the carriage, and this time they succeed at keeping me in. Pierre falls to his knees and watches as they take me away, tears streaming down his face. There is nothing he can do. My father watches him from where he stands and says nothing.

My father seems to fight back tears—he may have some sort of a heart deep down, despite his actions and temperament. He loves me, but he loves his reputation and social standing more. He isn't one to ever show any emotion, unless it is anger. It's as if fighting back the tears makes him angrier, and he tries to maintain his stern face as he heads inside with my mother.

I sit in the carriage, unable to get out. The door has been locked from the outside. The fear starts to set in. I don't know where I am being taken; I can only assume the worst. I'm still wearing my clothes from the night before, and my sandy bare feet are cold against the wooden floor of the carriage. The road is anything but smooth. I know my father is one to hand out severe punishments. I say a silent prayer for God to help me as I await my destination in anguish.

The carriage finally comes to a stop after what seems like an eternity on the roads. My hands begin to tremble, as I cannot be too sure what awaits me.

A man yanks open the carriage door. "Let's go!" he says sternly.

We are at a dock, and there are tall ships waiting to leave. Still trembling, with tear-filled eyes, I hesitate to walk forward.

"Where are we going?" I ask, and my voice cracks.

"There's no we. It's just *you*. Your father is exiling you to England. There, a family friend will pick you up, and you will remain with them. You will see your accommodations are generous. Safe travels."

I am guided to my quarters, and for the entire voyage, I hardly leave my room. I spend almost all of it crying. All I can think of is that I will never see my family again; nor will I see Pierre. Despite everything, I still love him very much, and I hope someday we can see each other again and live out our love. But it is futile to think such wishes will ever happen. *I must move on*, I tell myself.

The ship arrives in London after a month or so at sea. I have gotten so used to the ocean's movements that I hardly notice it anymore. What once made me feel sick now soothes me to sleep.

I hear a knock at my door.

"Yes?" I call out.

"Miss, I am here to collect you. I come on behalf of the James family. You will be staying with us," the voice says politely.

I hesitate to open the door, still afraid of the whole ordeal.

"Miss?" the voice says again.

I take a deep breath and open it.

There stands a man with boyish looks, red hair, and bright blue eyes.

"Ah! There you are, miss! Lovely to see you. Are you all right? How was the trip here?"

"Under these circumstances . . . rocky," I say without emotion.

A nervous look comes over his face, as if he knows exactly what I am talking about. I'm assuming my father informed them all of everything.

"I am so sorry for what you have gone through, miss, but I just want to say you are more than welcome at the James home. They are delighted to have you," he says, trying to make me feel better and dissolve any awkwardness.

"Thank you," I say in almost a whisper.

"Come on, let's get going. They're expecting you," he says to me, and I look up at him. "My name is Andrew, by the way. I work for the James family."

"Nice to meet you, Andrew. I am Helena. Helena Bernabéu," I say, struggling to conjure up a small smile.

"What a lovely name! Nice to meet you, Helena," Andrew says back.

He loads my luggage onto the carriage, and we embark on our ride to the James estate.

I can't help but feel incredibly nervous. I don't know these people. I am in a whole new country I will be forced to call home, heading for a whole new family. Away from the people I love and everything I know. This is where my fear of the unknown originates from.

After several hours of traveling, we finally arrive. I peer outside the window to take a look, and the place just takes my breath away. It is grand and intimidating. I have to assume this family is royalty or, at the very least, connected to the royal family. The little shrubs in front of the steps to the main door almost appear fake; I can't detect any leaves that may be past their time. They're perfectly green. The stone chosen to build the home is white, lending the estate a castle-like appearance.

My eyes widen, struggling to take in the grandeur. How could anyone possibly get used to seeing this? The lawn surrounding the home is neatly kept, giving a beautiful contrast with the white stone of the place.

From where I stand, I can see a silhouette in one of the front windows; I assume it's on the second floor, but I can't be too sure. My interest is piqued, as I want to know who lives in such a place.

Andrew takes us up the driveway and stops in front of the main door. He politely opens the door for me. I take his hand and gently step out of the carriage.

The grand main door opens, and out comes a very elegant and beautiful woman.

"Why, hello, dear! You must be Helena. I am Mrs. James, but you can call me Victoria. We have been eagerly awaiting your arrival. I wish the circumstances were different, but nonetheless, we are happy to have you," she says to me warmly.

"Thank you," I say, a bit embarrassed that she knows everything. Mrs. James gives me a big, comforting hug.

"Come on, dear. You must meet the family. I have two sons—Emmett and Charles—and my husband, Sir Ashby, whom you will meet shortly. Oh! Thank you, Andrew, thank you. You're relieved of work for the rest of the day, dear."

"Thank you, ma'am," Andrew says politely. "Nice to meet you again, Helena! I'll see you around."

I smile and nod quickly as Mrs. James excitedly leads me up the stairs and into a magnificent entryway. She closes the door behind us and beckons me into the living room. The grand fireplace is the largest I've ever seen. I stand at about five foot four, and I could walk right into the fireplace perfectly without having to hunch down. I marvel at the ivory limestone used, and at the etched green ivy with white roses that adorns the mantel.

On the elegant couch lies an even more elegant man, a younger one, with beautiful thick black hair.

"Emmett," Mrs. James says, "Helena is here. Helena Bernabéu. Come say hello."

I stay beside Victoria, my arm interlocked with hers. Almost as if in slow motion, Emmett closes his book and puts it down on the couch as he rises to greet me. His soulful blue eyes meet my gaze, and it is as if time itself has stopped. He seems to blush but does his best to stay elegantly composed.

"Nice to meet you, Helena. I am Emmett James. Victoria's son," he says with a big smile, full of humor. "It is lovely to meet you, and if I may say so respectfully, you are absolutely gorgeous." He proceeds to take my hand and plant a kiss on it. "I hope you will like it here."

"Thank you," I say quietly, and probably also blushing at that unexpected compliment. My heart pounds in my chest just from looking at him—he is so beautiful. I'm surprised at how quickly I've taken a liking to Emmett. I wonder if I should try to keep my distance from him at first.

"Where is your father? And your brother?" Mrs. James asks Emmett.

"Ah, I believe Father is busy in his study with Sir Remy Gautier. He should be out in a moment. As for Charles, I don't know. Maybe outside in the rose garden?" he responds ever so eloquently.

I love the way Emmett speaks. His voice is deep, but gentle and warm. He is a very caring man. I will later learn that Emmett is about nine years older than me, unmarried, and looking for a wife—but not in a hurry, his mother will tell me. I have to wonder if she took notice of the energy between Emmett and I upon our meeting.

"Well, I will let you get settled in, dear. You can meet the rest of the family at dinner. Emmett, won't you show her where she will be staying?" Mrs. James says.

I become nervous as Emmett takes my hand and leads me upstairs. The house staff already took my luggage up to my bedroom as soon as I arrived.

Emmett seems to sense my nervousness. "I apologize for taking your hand in such a forward manner."

"It's quite all right," I say shyly.

"Your room is right across from mine, so if you ever need anything, I'm closest . . . I mean—" Emmett suddenly struggles with his words, only adding to the tension; his elegant composure is succumbing to the strong attraction between us.

I smile shyly once more as I realize the fluster and fascination is mutual.

"I'm sorry. I assure you I am not usually like this," he says, trying to regain control over himself.

I nod and look down at my feet, doing my best to relieve him of my gaze, because every time I look at him, he only becomes more flustered.

Emmett opens the door to my bedroom. It is very large and spacious. I have my own fireplace and a nice window nook overlooking the magnificent rose garden.

"It is very generous. Thank you," I say to him with a smile.

Emmett nods respectfully.

I gaze out the window to admire the garden. I can sense Emmett's blue eyes on me.

"I can show you around the grounds later on. Maybe after dinner?" he suggests.

"I'd love that." I look at him once more, and I can see the flustered emotions arise in him again.

"All right," he says, doing his best not to butcher his words. "I'll see you at dinner. Dinner is at seven, but someone will call for you, or you can just come downstairs."

I nod and try to stop myself from laughing; his nervousness is adorable.

Emmett closes my bedroom door behind him.

I sit by the window and take a deep breath, trying to take in everything outside. I notice another young man—about three years older than me—standing in the garden, surrounded by the red roses. He admires one and selects it, gently cutting it as he smells the rose carefully.

Unexpectedly, he looks up at my window, and both of us startle. I stay where I am, a bit embarrassed. He smiles at me. He is very handsome too; he looks a lot like Emmett, so I assume he must be his younger brother, Charles.

He continues smiling and nods in acknowledgment. I smile back, getting up from where I sit, and begin to unpack my belongings so that I will be settled in before dinner. Everyone at the James's home has been very kind to me. I have to be thankful for that. It could be far worse.

After unpacking, I lie down on the bed to rest, completely exhausted. In doing so, I miss dinner that evening, sleeping right on through the night. I dream of Pierre and our time together. I will never forget our love; my love for him is forever.

I awake the following morning to a knock at my door. I get up quickly and put my robe on over my nightdress.

I open the door to see Mrs. James standing before me.

"Good morning, dear. Did you sleep all right?" she asks.

"Yes, I did. Very well, thank you," I say back politely.

"I thought I'd bring you breakfast myself. You must be starved! You missed dinner yesterday."

"Yes, I just slept right on through," I say, letting her in with the breakfast tray.

She places the tray on the table in the sitting area by the fireplace. "We are going for a little walk around the grounds this morning, if you'd like to come. After you eat, of course."

"That is so kind, and yes, I would love that," I say, smiling. "Now that I am well rested, I think I am up for it."

"All right, dear. Just come downstairs when you are done eating and getting dressed. We won't leave without you," she says, seeing herself out.

She is very kind and warm. Emmett resembles his mother a lot. I hope Emmett will be there on the walk this morning. I'm looking forward to his friendship while I'm here. I quickly eat my breakfast and get dressed.

Emmett is the first person I see on my way down the stairs. His eyes meet mine, and we both look away quickly and awkwardly. Mrs. James rushes up to me and takes my arm. She interlocks her arm with mine.

"Come on, dear. We have much to see. Not in a hurry, of course, but the grounds are very vast."

"Are we not waiting for Charles?" Emmett asks his mother.

"Oh, Emmett, you know Charles sleeps in until noon. If we decide to wait for him, we will be here all morning!"

We go out the back through the garden.

Emmett follows behind us.

Chapter 10

“Your garden is magnificent, Mrs. James,” I say as I take a look around.

The garden complements the front of the estate incredibly well. The luscious green landscaping is everywhere. Different kinds of flowers abound, but the rose garden is the most wondrous. There are plenty of little wooden benches to sit wherever one would like among the greenery. It is an absolute sanctuary. The air is fresh, and the skies are bright blue. Everything is different here, vastly unlike anything I saw or experienced back home in Spain, though both are beautiful in their unique ways.

“Victoria. Please, call me Victoria.”

“All right, Victoria,” I say.

“It is my pride and joy, darling. If you can’t find me in the house, you can most certainly find me out here. I love roses, don’t you?” she asks as she admires one of the red roses.

“I do. The white rose is my absolute favorite,” I say happily.

Emmett quickly scans the rose garden for the most beautiful white rose and cuts it for me.

“For you,” he says, extending the rose out to me.

I can't help but be entranced by his gaze. His soulful blue eyes are magnetically enchanting in the dreamiest way.

"Thank you," I say, flustered by it all.

"Any reason in particular that one's your favorite?" Mrs. James continues.

"Besides it's infinite beauty, I just love the purity of the white color against the luscious green stem," I say, admiring the rose Emmett gifted me.

Mrs. James tries to pretend she isn't noticing what is going on between her eldest son and I, but I feel it is only a matter of time before she says something to me. We continue walking around the property, taking our time and enjoying the fresh air. Emmett stays beside me; being this close to him gives me butterflies. I can smell his cologne, subtle yet appealing. It isn't overpowering at all, but its seductive aroma makes it hard for me to concentrate and pay attention to what Mrs. James is telling me about the property. She goes on and on about the different sections of land and the family history.

Suddenly, someone from her staff comes running out, calling for her.

"Ma'am! Someone is here to see you."

Mrs. James nods back in acknowledgment. "All right, tell them I'll be there shortly. Emmett dear, keep Helena company?"

"Yes, go ahead. She's in good hands with me," Emmett says to his mother.

"All right. I will see you in a moment, Helena."

Mrs. James goes back to the house, leaving Emmett and me alone.

The tension is growing stronger. The more we are around each other, the more it is felt. The energy is potent, almost like a loaded gun waiting to fire.

"How do you like it here so far?" Emmett asks.

I let out a sigh while we continue walking. "It's lovely here. Very peaceful. You all have shown me such kindness in taking me in. This isn't easy or comfortable for me. So I just want to say thank you for understanding and showing sensitivity," I say, hating the vulnerable position I am in.

Emmett stops walking for a moment and looks at me. "I heard some of what happened, and I know it's none of my business. But I think what your father did, and is doing to you, is not right. I am sorry you're going through something like this. Falling in love is not a crime. He could've handled this in a more compassionate way."

I fight back tears, thinking about the unfairness in everything that has happened, but I just nod. Emmett pulls me close and holds me; his embrace feels like a cozy cashmere shawl that I never want to take off.

"You are safe here," he continues reassuring me softly. "You're safe with my family and me, and we will protect you. You don't have to worry about anything. It's going to be all right,"

Mrs. James sees us embrace from afar. She looks as though she doesn't quite know what to do, but maybe, I think, this is destiny's doing.

Catherine's voice starts to come into focus softly.

"I am going to bring you back now. Four, three, two, one, all the way. Slowly take your time to come back."

I start to leave Emmett's embrace and come back to the present.

I take my time and open my eyes, pulling in a deep breath. Then I slowly sit up to look at Catherine. "That was amazing!"

"Right?" she says, just as excited. "I wrote a lot of notes."

"Do the regressions fade?" I ask, concerned.

"Some patients have said that their memories do fade over time. But everyone is different. Just as a precaution, you should journal it. I highly recommend it."

"Okay," I say quietly.

Catherine smiles. "So, what do you think?" she asks, looking at me as she eagerly awaits my response.

"To say that my mind is blown is an understatement. I can't even put it all into words right now. It is going to take me a while to come to terms with all of this. This is all real! There is no way I am imagining this. This is insane! How do I even begin to process this? The warmth and familiarity between myself and the people I saw . . . I know some, but others I haven't known in this life. At least not yet. I could feel everything! My emotions for Emmett—upon seeing him, my soul just lit up. It made me feel as if I miss him. But how could I miss him without even knowing who he is, or was? So weird. And I saw Phillip, but he was named Pierre then."

I pause and shake my head. "I've always wanted to 'time travel,' and now here I am, feeling as if I have. I'm curious as to why the guides are showing me this time line. I can't help but wonder. All I know is that seeing them both back then makes me feel torn between the two."

"Oh, Jess is going to be excited to hear from you!" Catherine smiles at me, clearly giddy at the thought of me relaying to Jess what I just saw in the regression. "All right, same time tomorrow?"

"Yes! I am so eager to find out more about my past. What I have seen so far is very interesting. I want to know more. I want to know the full story of what happened," I say, unable to contain my curiosity.

"And you will. I promise you."

"The people I saw in my regression in England, I haven't met any of them in this life. Their souls didn't seem familiar," I say, confused. "But Pierre Martin . . . Pierre is Phillip. For sure!"

"When we meet people from our past, it is all in divine timing. It is all according to a divine plan that things unfold," Catherine says with wisdom. "We must learn to trust it, and sometimes we don't meet them in this lifetime. Sometimes it's future lives."

I nod, furrowing my brow as I ponder her words. "We have only been here two hours? I was able to see so much in two hours! It did not feel that long at all. It felt like five minutes."

"Time works a little different when you're regressed and how you're able to see things. I still don't understand it all, but that's just how I have seen it to be."

"Well, thank you so much. Thank you for being a part of my journey! I will see you again tomorrow, and we can continue this then," I say, standing up.

Catherine nods and guides me to the door. "No, thank you. Thank you for letting me be a part of it. I look forward to learning more about your story and seeing where the guides take us."

I smile and give her a hug. "Me too. I'll see you tomorrow!"

"See you tomorrow!" Catherine says cheerfully.

I get in my car and drive home, ecstatic and amazed at what I have experienced. I have to talk to Jess as soon as possible! She was right about everything. It's real. It's all real! Astrology was truly just the tip of the iceberg, and now I can't help but think how asleep I have been—how asleep we all have been to the truth. The very truth of what we are, of why we are here, of how life works. The truth that we are immortal souls.

We have many bodies, many faces, but we are the same soul as we grow and evolve throughout lifetimes. God is in all of us; that is why we have the power to create our own realities. He made us in his image. Therefore, we have some of his abilities, I now know. Life is our teacher. Whatever we struggle with in our lives, that is our personal test. Some of us are failing, and some of us are passing. In Helena's case, she failed to leave the past behind her and took her second chance at love for granted. Her lesson was to learn to let go of Pierre and embrace her future with Emmett. But she didn't, becoming entangled and confused with her past and future. She was indecisive and failed to see how her actions could lead to disastrous pain for others, and for herself in the process.

If you don't learn your lesson in this lifetime, you keep repeating it over and over in future lifetimes. It's like repeating a grade in school because you're not grasping the material, and if you refuse to learn the lesson, your lifetimes will get harder and harder until you do. Knowing what I know now, I want to scream it from the rooftops. I want to scream at everyone I come across now and say, *Wake up! Wake up to the truth! Or look into it for yourself, and you will see.*

Now I understand completely why Jess wouldn't shut up about it. Once you open your eyes to the truth, there is no closing them again. Your whole perspective on life changes, on the answer to why we are here. What is the purpose of life? Death can no longer be called death but rather ascension. When we "die," we ascend into a higher realm. We never truly die! Our consciousness goes on. The whole purpose of us returning is to continue to learn, like Helena.

Many people fail to learn and evolve. Each soul's lesson is different, and for some people, their teacher is the loss itself. Some choose to focus on what they lost instead of what they still have around them. They forget about all the good and let the pain of loss overtake them, and they waste their time on Earth, blinded by their loss. They don't become aware that they lost sight of the big picture until after they ascend.

That is just one example of why a soul would return after ascension—to expand their consciousness. Life gives us many chances to get things right and evolve into our higher selves. A soul assigned the lesson of loss will keep repeating the same circumstances until they "wake up" to the pattern that continues to unfold before them. They will become aware that the loss is trying to teach them to cherish what they do have, when they have it. Nothing can ever truly be possessed forever anyway; it is in learning to let go that they can be at peace. Control is an illusion.

Taking all of this new knowledge in, I make it down to Scenic Drive. I pull into my driveway and realize that the drive seemed shorter than usual, probably because my head was lost in my obsessive thinking. I am going to call it a day. I'm very sleepy and think it would be best to tell Jess everything in person anyway. There is just too much detail, and it would be hard to explain over text or a phone call.

To my surprise, I find myself falling into a deep sleep rather quickly in my bedroom. My mind is always very active, and I have a hard time falling asleep. Usually I am up writing at night; that is when inspiration strikes. As I lie in bed and drift off to sleep, feeling my conscious mind fade and my subconscious mind emerge, I begin to dream.

In the dream I am getting up from my bed and walking down my stairs. I am going through my living room and out my front door. I can hear the roar of the ocean waves crashing on the shore across the street. The night sky looks breathtaking; the air is cold against my skin. The foggy mist of the ocean makes my hair and skin damp. I breathe in the fresh air. I can feel the coldness in my chest.

I look around and see no one; the serenity of the night is seductive. I walk across the street and down the wooden steps that lead to the beach, and my bare feet imprint into the wintry sand. I begin to hear whispers, but I struggle to make anything out. I keep walking toward the water. Suddenly, a glowing light emerges before me. It floats just above the ocean waves. It begins to speak. Its powerful voice vibrates with high energy. I can feel it in my bones.

"What happened then, what is happening now, and what is yet to happen . . . is all meant to be, for it is your destiny. Don't run from it. Don't fear it, for I am with you always, guiding and protecting you. As you listen carefully to my messages, I will send you many more. The number sequences will increase. I will reach you through song, and I will reach you through the people who come into your life. Hear my words carefully. All is well, and all is as it should be."

"What?" I say, confused. "What are you? What is happening? Hello! Hello?" I shout, but the light vanishes before my eyes.

I wake up from my dream and find myself lying on the beach with the sun shining brightly. A man walks over to me to see if I am okay.

"Hello?" he calls out to me. "Are you all right? You were shouting in your sleep."

I look up at him, confused. "What happened? Why am I out here?"

He smiles, just as puzzled. "I was hoping you'd tell me that. Where do you live?"

I point to my home across the way and start to make my way back.

"Take care of yourself!" he says to me.

I run across the sand, feeling as if my heart is in my throat. Fear courses through my veins. Something is happening, and I can't figure out exactly what it is. I could've sworn it was a dream. Was I dreaming? Maybe sleepwalking?

Fear begins to consume my thoughts. I text Jess and tell her to come to my house immediately. I need to tell her what happened.

I've been so caught up in what happened that I only just now realize that Phillip didn't come home last night. I check my phone before getting in the shower, but there aren't any messages from him. As soon as I finish my shower and get dressed, I hear a knock at my front door. I run downstairs and look through the window to check who it is before I open it. Seeing that it is Jess, I swing the door open immediately.

"Come in! Hurry!" I say frantically.

She takes a seat in the living room, looking a little confused.

"What happened? How did it go?" she asks.

"Okay, first of all, are there any side effects to undergoing these regressions?" I ask her assertively.

A concerned expression comes over her face. "What do you mean?"

"Just answer the damn question." My heart is racing so fast I can hear my pulse in my ears.

"Oh my god! No, I've never experienced any. I know there are people who say they sleep better and that their fear of death goes away . . . but I take it that's not the case with you? What happened?" Jess asks again, more concerned.

"I woke up on the fucking beach this morning! Without any clue as to how the fuck I got out there! I thought I was dreaming! I thought it was a dream! And I wake up on the fucking beach after some bright-lighted being was floating in front of me speaking in riddles!"

"Wait, what?" Jess asks. "Hold on. . . . You were sleepwalking?"

I roll my eyes and pour us some coffee that I made before entering the shower. "I don't know. Is that what sleepwalking is? Me crossing my street onto the beach in the dark of night? And I think I'm asleep in my bed and I'm not? And some bright-lighted thing comes and speaks to me? I don't know. I really, really don't know, but it is scaring the shit out of me. What is this?" I am unable to keep my cool.

"Calm down. Maybe you can ask Catherine. Maybe she knows someone who has had this kind of experience. I mean, it sounds like sleepwalking. . . . The timing is just very interesting. What did this thing you're talking about say to you? Do you remember?"

I take a deep breath and sit down on the couch. Closing my eyes, I try to remember word for word what he said. "Something about what happened then and what is happening now and what is yet to happen is all meant to be. I am with you, guiding and protecting. I will reach you through song. I will reach you through people who come into your life. The number sequences will only increase as you receive my messages, and I will send you many more. All is well. . . . I think that is all of it? Just off the top of my mind and what I can remember."

Jess's eyes grow wide with excitement. "What if you're having an out-of-body experience? These things happen!"

"Oh, come on! Are you serious?" I say, annoyed. "Are you even taking this seriously? I'm afraid over here! And you're excited?"

"Maybe it was your spirit guide communicating with you somehow? Through your dreams? I mean, you are gifted. You just don't own it," Jess says. "You are in the early stages of embracing it! Now that you have finally allowed the spiritual in, this happens? Think about it!"

She proceeds to take a sip from her coffee and groans. "Oh shit, this is bitter! Where's the creamer?"

I smile and point at the fridge.

I lie down on the couch and think over what Jess is saying. I have always been intuitive and somewhat gifted. I can pick up on energies from people and places. I just know how things will play out when I focus on the situation. But I never thought anything of it, and I certainly didn't think something of this magnitude could ever happen to me. I am not certain if I am clairvoyant. All I know is it isn't something I find easy to embrace—given my conservative and by-the-book religious upbringing taught me that psychics, or really anything of that nature, are evil. It's hard to let go of old beliefs.

Jess, now content with her coffee, sits down beside me. "I think you're becoming who you are meant to be, and the universe is forcing you to embrace it."

I let out a disgruntled sigh. "You really think so? I mean, you're not at all afraid?"

"Should you be cautious? Yes! But you're spiritual. You're gifted. You are different from your family, and they are always going to fear what they don't understand. I honestly mean it when I say I think you are becoming who you are meant to be, and that can be scary. This is your North Node, your soul mission. That is why you feel the fear! It is unknown territory to your soul," Jess says, nudging me playfully.

"Okay . . ." I say with another sigh. "We will see if it happens again. I will keep you posted."

Jess sips her coffee loudly on purpose to annoy me. "So, what else happened? Is that all?"

I give her a death stare. "Is that all? Really? Oh, it isn't much for you?"

"No, I just mean did anything else happen? I want to know!" she says enthusiastically.

"You're mocking me, aren't you?" I ask, unamused by her demeanor.

"No, I'm serious!" Jess insists. "Why would I mock you?"

"Can you stay with me all day? I don't want to be alone right now, and Phillip didn't come home last night."

"You? *You* don't want to be alone? Aren't you, like, the ultimate lone wolf who loves her own company?" she says, smiling at me.

"Yes, but not right now."

"Wait, what do you mean Phillip didn't come home last night? Does he usually do that?" Jess asks.

"I mean . . . he's swamped with work. He works a ton. He promised he'd slow down once we are ready to start growing our family. That reminds me, I didn't tell you about what I saw in my regression. I saw Phillip. He was a love interest—my love interest in that life. I haven't gotten the full story yet, since it was just my first session," I say rapidly.

Jess almost chokes on her coffee.

Chapter 11

"Yes," I continue, relating the story of my first regression to a past life. "It's true. Phillip—who was called Pierre Martin—and I loved each other very much, but we were separated by my father. It was in the eighteenth century. In that life I was sent away from my family in Spain to live with another family in England as punishment."

Jess's expression is that of a child, filled with wonder, but she says nothing, allowing me to continue.

"The last thing I was shown was the other family I was sent to live with in England. I didn't recognize any of them. I had a strong connection from the beginning with one of them. A very handsome Englishman, actually. His name was Emmett James."

At this point Jess is just enchanted with the details I relay to her. "This is so cool! When is your next session?"

"Today, after class," I say. "Do you think it is possible that I may run into Emmett again one day—I mean now, in my current life?"

Jess thinks for a moment. "Yeah, I don't see why not," she finally says. "I mean, you're now married to Phillip, who you're saying was Pierre Martin in that other life, right? So yeah. Maybe?"

"Maybe as friends this time though, right? Since I am married to Phillip," I say, losing myself in the thought for a moment.

"Who knows? That's if he even chose to incarnate in this lifetime," Jess adds.

"That would be so crazy! And what if I could . . . Let's say upon meeting him, I would feel something, right? Some sort of familiarity," I ponder aloud. "And I can see his birth chart and put it together with mine? And be able to fact check everything in a way, right?"

She nods in agreement. "Yeah, you can start your little web of research. You have your half of the map. You would just need to check his, but what if he were reincarnated as a girl? Fate has its own design and agenda. Maybe in this life, you are not meant to cross paths? I've seen that happen, where two people who have been together before find each other again, only to find out that fate and destiny have other plans." She pauses for a moment. "It can be heartbreaking."

"Wow. That comment came out of left field! Pessimism. Are you feeling a little blue? I can take my own pessimism, but not yours," I tell her.

Jess smiles. "All right, I'm just saying. You don't know what fate has designed," she says with a shrug. "Come on, we have to get going. I have a class to teach. And you have a class to *attend*."

In class, I pay extra close attention to the material as Jess explains it to all of us. I find myself eager to apply it in deciphering more about the past life. Jess has us all do an exercise where we hand the person next to us our chart and they try to read it just by looking at it, without looking up anything. Amelia, another student, sits beside me and begins reading my chart, while I read Jason's, the man who's sitting on the other side of me.

I finish within fifteen minutes.

"You got it?" Jess asks.

"Yup."

Everyone else looks up at me.

"All right, what did you find?" Jason asks.

I begin with his South Node and go into detail about his past life that is being brought forward into this one, combining with how it manifests into his personality. Then, I continue with his North Node and do the same thing, eloquently explaining everything. The look on his face is hysterical, and Jess looks over my shoulder at his chart and nods in agreement at everything I am saying. I explain that when I read an astrological birth chart, I do so by starting with the Nodes of the moon, simply because everyone wants to know what we are here to do. What is our soul mission? I try to answer that from the beginning. Knowing what you agreed to come back here on Earth for is, in my opinion, the most important. I start to mention some of Jason's shortcomings and how some of his relationships might play out. At that point he begins to get very uncomfortable with how accurate the information is.

"Okay, umm . . . let me just say I feel personally attacked right now," he says, blushing. "Please stop!"

I look up. I forgot that while I am looking at someone's birth chart, I have to remember to be sensitive in my delivery of words. I can't be so cold and analytical, as if I am studying an experiment. People don't like being looked into or feeling vulnerable. I count myself in that too.

"I'm sorry if I made you uncomfortable," I say to Jason genuinely.

"Well, I mean, you should take it as a compliment. You're good. Everything you were saying was spot-on accurate! And you deciphered it and read it so fast!" he says, still blushing. "I feel like you were looking into my very soul."

Everyone at the table smiles at his reaction.

Jess ends the class with a valuable message. "Reading astrological birth charts can be that way. They are a great tool to find out what you are here to do. They can also be used to see where your shortcomings are and strengths. This is why it is imperative to be sensitive in the delivery of your words and when deciphering someone's chart. The sole purpose of learning this material is so you can hopefully use it for good, to help and guide people to better themselves—and ultimately help them along the way to accomplish their soul mission."

I nod as my teacher, Jess, voices what I was already thinking.

Two Paths Become One

Chapter 12

Taking quickly to life in Carmel-by-the-Sea, Emery starts to decorate his new home. He is excited to begin fresh somewhere new, and he is glad it ended up being in such a lovely little seaside town. He decides to make a trip to the grocery store to buy a couple of things. He wants to cook dinner for himself in his new state-of-the-art kitchen, relishing his newfound freedom. He likes that no one knows his name here, and paparazzi don't lie in wait outside every time he ventures out of his house.

Upon entering the store's wine aisle, he notices a woman he deems familiar. Emery takes his time exploring the wine selection and occasionally glances at the woman. Suddenly he realizes that it is Catherine Jennings, the well-known psychologist and author whose event he is going to—the very reason he moved here in the first place. He does his best not to lose his cool and approaches her.

"Hello, I hate to bother you, but you're Catherine Jennings. Correct?" Emery asks.

Catherine's green eyes turn to look at Emery. "Yes, I am," she says with a warm smile.

"I am attending your event this week! I read your book about past-life regressions, and I loved it!" Emery says to her excitedly.

"Thank you so much. Are you really coming? That's awesome!" she says, almost giddy with delight. "Have you had a regression done yet?"

Emery smiles from ear to ear. "I have, actually! I have discovered quite a bit so far from a particular past life. I have actually been able to find some physical things, like a portrait miniature and other stuff."

Catherine's eyes grow wide with excitement. "Wow! That is incredible!" she says, smiling. "You would think that after all these years, I would be immune to this excitement of people's past-life discoveries! But nope, it feels like the first time every time!"

"It truly is for me," Emery says. "I have only just begun. I have only had one session done and am dying to have another. I want to figure out the rest of the story! My mother is the one I did my regression with, but she's in England, and I am just settling in here for a while. So I don't know when I will get another chance."

"I would be more than happy to help you with that, if you'd like," Catherine offers graciously.

They both begin to walk out of the wine aisle and into the produce section, still chatting away.

Catherine hands Emery her business card. "Here is my contact info. Feel free to reach out to me when you have the time, and I can pencil you in to my schedule."

Emery takes the card from Catherine happily. "Thank you so much! I most definitely will!"

"Well, I am about done with my shopping. I will see you at my event in a few days, Emery!" Catherine says.

Emery nods and waves goodbye. "It was lovely talking to you."

Emery proceeds to finish up his shopping for dinner and heads home, still excited about having run into Catherine at the store. What are the odds?

He takes Catherine up on her offer and agrees to see her regularly for regressions. At their first meeting, he is charmed by her office. He walks up the steps and knocks on the door. Feeling eerily relaxed, he remembers what he saw on his past regression with his mother and hopes maybe he can see more today.

The door swings open slowly.

"Hi, Emery! Come on in," Catherine says warmly.

"How are you?" Emery asks, walking in.

"Good. Busy, but good. Full schedule as of late." She puts her glasses on and signals for him to have a seat on the couch. Then she sits right across from him. "It always gets this way before an event, usually a lot of my patients want to get a regression done. It makes conversations more intriguing; people like to mingle and share their stories."

Emery listens quietly, gazing at Catherine, ready to begin.

"All right," Catherine says, "so I want to begin by asking a few questions for my notes, just to kind of play catch up, since you have already had one session. What have you seen so far in that first regression?"

Emery takes a deep breath. "Well, I was a wealthy man from a prestigious and distinguished family in the eighteenth century, in England. My name was Emmett James. I was married to a woman named Helena. I felt my love for her. It was overwhelming, but she betrayed me. She was unfaithful, and I killed the man she had an affair with. That is what I have seen thus far."

Catherine writes some of it down and then pauses and looks up at Emery slowly. She doesn't say a word, but her stunned silence piques Emery's interest.

"Catherine?" he says, intently watching her.

"*Helena* is what you said?" she asks.

"Yes, why?"

Catherine seems to be withholding something. Emery's heart begins to race with anticipation. What if she knows something about his past life—or even about Helena, whose name clearly grabbed her attention?

"Catherine," he says, "you look as though something I said sounds familiar. Do you know something you want to share with me?"

She puts down her pen and sighs. "That is for another time. I don't want to speak prematurely. Let's just stay with your story, and let's begin."

Emery nods and lies down on the couch.

As Catherine begins her process of hypnosis, it isn't long before Emery enters a deep state of relaxation. The guides show him everything.

Emery finds himself once again as Emmett James, and right away he sees Helena, his wife. His emotions for her again overwhelm him with such passion. It is as if an oceanic storm surges in his chest. Tears fill his eyes.

"They tell me I need to heal. I need to heal from this pain," Emery says, his voice shaking. The tears begin to stream down the sides of his face.

Emery is then shown Pierre Martin, and again feelings of murderous rage arise in his heart. "He loved her too, and he didn't want to let her go. He never has let her go, and he never will. Nor will I."

Emery sees that his family in that life is the same group of souls in this one. He smiles upon seeing his mother there in that life with him. Their bond is ever prominent. His guides show him how everything unfolded, withholding nothing. He relives the pain of Helena's betrayal.

"Detach and float above the scene if you must," Catherine says softly.

But the guides won't let him. Suddenly the guides begin to speak through Emery to Catherine.

"Emmett must remember what happened," Emery says, conveying the guides' message. "He must remember what he did in that life cycle. Things that happened then must not repeat themselves, for if so, they will forever stay in that circle of karma."

As he says this, a scene unfolds before him, much like a movie. He—as Emmett James—is standing in the grand living room of the James estate. Looking out the window to the rose garden, he is aware his wife, Helena, hasn't arrived home from her trip into London. He received word that she was seen at Pierre Martin's estate, alone.

Once more, he is immersed in the scene as his former self. He tries to keep his emotions in check, but he can't. His heart pulses with anger, and he fears the worst. He paces back and forth restlessly.

"She wouldn't," he mutters to himself. "She wouldn't betray me." Emmett looks down at his trembling hands. He pours himself a drink and sits down on the sofa in front of the fireplace.

Not long after, Helena finally arrives back home. He can see her from where he sits. She sees Emmett too but avoids looking at him and runs upstairs to their bedroom. Her behavior brings out the worst in Emmett as it fuels his suspicions. He runs up the stairs after her and bursts into the room, startling Helena.

"Where have you been?" Emmett demands.

"In London," she answers back quickly, but her gaze is different. Emmett sees the fear in her eyes.

"Why do I sense that your demeanor toward me has suddenly changed?" he asks boldly.

"Emmett, I don't know what you're talking about," Helena says, deflecting any emotion, but this only enrages Emmett further.

"Do you take me for a fool?" Emmett asks her. His tone of voice changes, and Helena can see that Emmett knows something. Perhaps she fears someone saw her at Pierre Martin's estate and relayed that information to Emmett. The tension between them increases. He boldly asks her straight out, "Did you visit Pierre Martin? Did you seek him out?"

Helena looks away. Her avoidance confirms his suspicions. Tears fill her eyes as she looks at Emmett. He watches the tears fall.

From that point, an uncontrollable rage overtakes him. "What happened?" he shouts angrily at Helena. She tries to get away from him, but Emmett quickly slams the door to their bedroom. Putting his hands on the sides of her face, he pulls her toward him.

"Tell me!" he shouts. His piercing gaze, once filled with love for her, is now consumed with rage and deep hurt.

"Emmett," she struggles to say, "please. Let me go."

But he pulls her in tighter. "Not until you tell me. I already know you went to see Pierre Martin. What *else* happened?" he asks. "I highly doubt you went to discuss business, considering your past together."

Helena stays quiet, as if in fear of what Emmett might do if he finds out everything. However, given her reaction to his suspicions alone, he was right on the mark.

"Tell me!" he shouts again. Angry tears fill his eyes. "Your silence and demeanor say it all, don't they? If nothing happened, if *you* had nothing to hide, if you were a *faithful* wife, you would not be acting this way!"

Helena begins to cry, and it only fuels Emmett's hostility. He throws her onto their bed forcefully.

"Emmett! Please stop!" Helena pleads.

"Not until you answer me!" Emmett shouts, pinning her on the bed.

Helena struggles to speak but cannot.

"Helena! I am only going to ask one more time," he warns. "What happened?"

He pulls himself off of her to try and calm down and then walks over to the bedroom's balcony and looks out to the green landscape of their estate, waiting. He quivers as he turns back to look at his wife, bracing for the truth. He stares at the ring on her left hand, the one that he proposed to her with. It is a massive and mesmerizing emerald shimmering on a dainty solid-gold band, symbolizing the promise of his love and devotion to her.

Helena can't find the courage to speak. She struggles through her tears to say, "I did go see Pierre at his home on my way back from my trip to London."

Emmett's eyes meet Helena's. "What did you go see him about? Did you lie with him?"

Helena begins to fidget with her hands.

"Stop fidgeting and answer the damn question!"

"Emmett . . . ," Helena mumbles. Her voice shakes as she struggles to get the words out. "I did," she finally answers. "Yes."

Emmett flips the coffee table in their room furiously. He lifts his hand to strike Helena across the face but stops himself halfway. Tears fill his eyes, making it difficult to see Helena's face clearly anymore. "Better yet . . . ," he says through his tears. Emmett puts on his silk banyan robe and races downstairs to the stables.

"Emmett!" Helena shouts helplessly.

She makes her way down the stairs after Emmett. She hears the galloping hooves of a horse and goes out to the front of their home. Emmett is riding off like a bat out of Hell, away from the estate.

"Emmett!" she shouts in despair.

Emmett races off to Pierre Martin's estate with his personal handgun. He can't believe Helena would hurt him like this. And he is prepared to do the unspeakable.

He arrives at Pierre's home and forces his way in. Pierre's housekeeper struggles to stop him at the door. She can see Emmett is extremely hostile, and she knows very well what he must be there for. She knows about Pierre and Helena, and now she realizes Emmett must also know.

"Sir, please wait here! I will go get Pierre for you. Please calm down!" she pleads with him, but Emmett isn't waiting for anyone.

"Pierre!" Emmett shouts angrily, his voice echoing throughout the home. He goes up the stairs and looks around for him but doesn't find him.

"Pierre!" he shouts again. He wanders into Pierre's room but finds it empty. He recognizes Helena's hair comb that she wears often on his bed, enraging him further. Emmett goes back downstairs.

"Where is he?" he shouts at Pierre's housekeeper.

"Please calm down, sir. If you are here to start trouble, please leave!" she pleads but fails to reason with him.

Emmett forces his way out to the garden and sees Pierre admiring a white rose, his back to Emmett.

"Pierre!" Emmett shouts, pulling out the gun and pointing it directly at him.

Pierre turns around, startled to see Emmett standing behind him with his flintlock pistol drawn. He puts his hands up, but before he can try to calm Emmett, the gun goes off.

Emmett fires at Pierre, killing him instantly.

Pierre falls to the ground, his body now lying lifeless on the grass. The white rose, now stained with Pierre's blood, still rests in his hand. His staff scream in horror at what has just occurred.

Emmett has done what he set out to do and rides back home.

Emery is almost jolted out of hypnosis as the magnitude of the memory throws him off. Catherine slowly brings him back to a full state of consciousness.

His first session with her is done. He takes a deep breath, opens his eyes, wipes away any residual tears, and turns to look at Catherine.

"That sounded intense," Catherine says to him.

Emery nods. "Yes, yes it was. The emotions were incredibly ardent." He turns his gaze down to his hands. Reliving the past with such depth—specifically those moments that have marked his soul for eternity—has rocked him to his core.

"I loved her," Emery says in almost a whisper, "and I still do. The love I feel for her will never die. I think when—if—I ever see her again, the magnitude of my feelings for her will affect me deeply and stronger than ever before. Every time is like the first time." His words validate what his soul already knew but his mind struggled to comprehend.

Catherine doesn't say much, preferring just to listen.

"I don't think it is any coincidence that I am here, is it?" Emery continues. "Fate, or destiny, is the reason why I am here. Our paths were meant to cross, Catherine. Part of me, to some small degree, used to hold some disdain for this stuff, but not anymore."

Catherine smiles at Emery. "Fate definitely has its hand in this. It is something that, if we choose to listen and follow, can lead us to our destiny. Sometimes destiny is a mission to help humanity collectively, and other times, our destiny could be wrapped up in one person."

Catherine pauses and glances down at her notes, looking thoughtful. "Emery, I think you came back here because you have unfinished business. When it comes to matters of the heart, it seems to me that this woman—your wife in that lifetime—is a part of your destiny now, in this life."

Emery's eyes gleam with wonder at the possibility. "If the guides are showing me this, then she very well could be reincarnated in this time frame with me. I guess it's only a matter of time before we run into each other, right?"

Catherine nods, but it looks to Emery as though she's not divulging all that she knows.

Emery goes to grab a drink later that night at the hotel he was staying at previously. The place is busy, and he takes a seat at the bar and orders his drink. The bartender quickly glances at Emery and smiles.

"You new around here?" he asks.

"Is it that obvious?" Emery answers calmly.

"I've never seen you before, and obviously the accent isn't from around here," the bartender says with a big smile. "So I guess that answers my question."

Emery smirks and nods. "Yeah, I'm from London. Just moved here."

They introduce themselves to each other, and the bartender asks Emery what brought him from London to California.

Emery looks down at his drink and then back at the bartender.

"Destiny," he says. He raises his glass and smiles.

After the hotel bar closes, Emery walks home. When he gets down to Scenic Drive, the cool ocean breeze blows against his warm skin. It feels good after a couple of drinks. The alcohol courses through his veins, causing him to feel drowsy, but he decides to sit on the beach for a moment. He stumbles slightly through the sand. It is hard for him to see, as the only light is the moonlight, and even that is faint.

Emery sits down on the sand and lets out a contented sigh. He is feeling freer than he ever has in his life. The ocean waves crash on the beach, and suddenly he hears a noise. Emery turns back to see what it may be. His drowsy drunkenness makes it hard for him to see who it is from a distance, but after a few moments, the moonlight illuminates the silhouette; it is a woman. He imagines she too is out to enjoy the night. Emery watches her from afar, thankful the faint street lights allow him to see her from where he sits, though he does his best to be discreet. There is something captivating about her.

The woman finally turns to look his way. She smiles politely and begins to walk down the beach past Emery. As she gets closer, he can see her more clearly.

"Him," she says to Emery as she walks by. She stops. Her face looks as if she's seen a ghost. They stare at each other for a moment without saying anything.

But Emery also feels he's seeing something unusual. Still sitting on the sand, he gazes at her and struggles to speak. He swallows deep and shallow as his heart begins to beat harder and faster, as though it is going to jump out of his chest and onto the sand.

The woman on the beach looks just like Helena.

"Hi . . . hello," he struggles to say aloud.

"It's a beautiful night, isn't it?" the woman says, perhaps attempting to play off her startled reaction to Emery.

"It is. It is indeed," Emery says, stammering and struggling to keep his cool. He watches her intently. "Are you from here?"

"I am," she answers back. "I live right across the street. And you?"

Emery stands and accompanies her as she walks beside the water. "I just moved here, actually. I live across the street too," he says, admiring her beauty. His soul feels alive just looking at her. He has a strange feeling that he's just found someone he's been looking for. But he knows that's unlikely, because he's only just figuring out who he's looking for: his true love, Helena, who could be anywhere in the world and anywhere in time. Still, there's something absolutely magnetic about this woman.

"Really?" she says. "So we're neighbors? Are you the one who bought the home three houses down from mine?"

"Yes, that's me. I'm the new guy in town." Emery chuckles.

She nods and looks down at her bare feet on the sand. "Well, it was nice meeting you, 'new guy in town.' I must go now," she says with a smile. "See you around!"

As she begins to walk away, Emery can't help himself.

"Wait! I didn't even ask your name," he says quickly.

She looks back at him. "Rose. And you are?"

"Emery. Emery Williams," he says, his eyes locked on hers. The moonlight illuminates her face ever so slightly, and he is completely hypnotized.

"Nice to meet you, Emery. Have a nice night, neighbor." Rose adjusts her head scarf and walks away in the direction of her home.

Emery nods and watches her leave. He is at a loss for words. He places his hand on his chest, feeling his heartbeat pound. Could this be *her*? He ponders what has just transpired. He thinks, *Destiny has brought me here. Fate whispered to me through people, circumstances, ideas, inspired action. Did all that lead me closer to her?*

Emery looks up to the night sky and smiles.

Chapter 13

As I remove my headscarf upon entering my home, my mind seems to be racing a thousand miles per hour. I am breathing heavily, but I can't catch my breath. I try to process what just happened, the man I stumbled into—Emery, he said was his name. He looks just like Emmett—exactly like the husband I remember from my past. He's English too! The way he looked at me was as if he had seen a ghost. I am in total shock, and I need to speak to Catherine Jennings as soon as possible.

As consumed as I am with my inner dialogue and my encounter with Emery, I don't realize immediately that my fireplace is on, and my husband, Phillip, is sitting on the sofa in front of the fireplace—with a nervous look on his face.

"Hi," I say to him, a bit unnerved.

"Are you all right?" he asks, concerned. "Did you even see me when you walked in?"

"I wasn't expecting you to be here," I say, trying to control my franticness. "Are you off work?"

"Yes, finally," Phillip says. "What's wrong? Has something happened?"

"No, I just . . . nothing," I say. "Forget about it. You've been gone a lot for work. I feel like I haven't seen you in weeks." I want to steer the subject away from what just happened to me on the beach.

"Yeah . . . about that. I'm sorry. I truly am. I've been carrying all the workload at my medical practice, and I know I've neglected you and our marriage. I'm trying to hire another doctor to help, but it's taking longer than I anticipated. Turns out good doctors are hard to come by."

I nod, but I feel lousy inside, lousy about us and our future together. Finally, I say, "I just don't know if this is sustainable."

"Come sit with me," Phillip says, making room for me on the sofa.

Hesitantly, I sit down beside him. We smile at each other like strangers would when passing each other on the street.

"I have given that a lot of thought too. Whether this marriage is sustainable or not. I love you very much," Phillip says, looking at me with such loving eyes. "I want this to work, I really do. I know we have been away from each other far too long."

I turn to stare at the flames in the fireplace, feeling disconnected and distracted. "I don't want to talk about this right now."

"What do you mean? We need to talk," Phillip says.

"Phillip, I just really need to text my therapist. There is something I need to tell her. We can talk in a bit. I just need to get my phone," I say with urgency.

Phillip stares at me, looking unsure of what to think. "All right. I'll make us some cappuccinos." He walks over to the kitchen and gets the espresso machine going.

I run up the stairs and grab my phone. Sitting on my bed, I call

Catherine. I anxiously wait while the phone rings. After about four rings, the call goes to voice mail. I leave her a message telling her about the man on the beach, Emery, and asking her to call me back as soon as she can.

I can hear Phillip just about to finish frothing the milk for the cappuccinos, and I make my way back down to the living room. "What if we sat up on the widow's peak so we can look out to the ocean?" I suggest.

"I was just about to say that!" he says, delighted, holding the drinks. "After you."

I lead the way to the widow's peak, and we get settled in on the cloudlike sofas.

"How have you been?" I ask.

Phillip looks out to the beach and then back at me. "Okay, I guess. . . . I know I haven't been prioritizing time together, and I've missed you. I hope it isn't too late. I want to make sure we are good, that we're talking about stuff."

I take a sip of my cappuccino but can't bring myself to smile or act as though our relationship is great, because it isn't.

"Is everything all right?" he asks. "You seem so distracted. Like you are here with me physically, but mentally you are someplace else."

Phillip's vibrant green eyes look at me, full of concern, as he waits for my response.

"I don't know what you want me to say," I answer, slightly annoyed. "I could say the same to you."

Phillip and I stare at each other for a few seconds without saying anything. The awkward silence fills the space between us.

"You're seeing a therapist?" he asks.

"Yup," I say, looking away.

"About us?"

"No. Not about us. About me."

"Oh," Phillip says, inviting another awkward silence in. "Can I ask why you were in a hurry to speak with her tonight? I mean . . . did something happen or . . . ?"

"It's hard to explain. Please don't press any further, Phillip."

Phillip nods. "All right," he says, confused, but he complies nonetheless. "I just feel like we need to talk. I have been working so much, and I feel bad. I leave you here alone, and I haven't been a good husband to you. I want to apologize again. I mean it when I say I want this to work."

"It's okay, Phillip. I get it. You work. People have to work. It's not a big deal," I say, brushing it off.

"It is a big deal! I love you. You have always been incredibly understanding with me and my work, and I want to thank you for your patience," he continues. "So I booked us a trip to Big Sur to reconnect and work on us."

Phillip sits beside me and pulls out the hotel information from his pocket to show me.

"Cool, I love Big Sur," I say, trying to muster up some enthusiasm.

I give Phillip a hug, but as I embrace him, Emery comes to mind once more. Ever since we crossed paths on the beach, I've felt as if my energy has shifted, and I can't control it. Something is happening or is about to happen, and I can feel it. And for that, I am excited. But also terribly scared.

The following morning, while I'm taking a quick shower, I hear a soft knock on the bathroom door.

"Honey?" Phillip says from the other side. "Honey?"

My eyes are still closed as I rinse out the shampoo from my hair, but I finally answer. "Yes? What is it?"

"You have a missed call. I think it's from your therapist . . ."

"Oh, okay. Thank you!" I say, finishing up.

Phillip lingers for a moment. I open the door for him just as he's about to knock again.

"Yes?" I ask, confused, wrapping the towel around myself.

"Nothing . . . you just look good," he says, smiling.

I quickly grab my phone and see that Catherine, in fact, did call. I hold off on returning her call, since Phillip is within earshot.

"What do you want to do today?" Phillip asks.

I walk into my closet, lost in thought, and I fail to hear him.

"Honey?" he says.

"What?" I say to him, completely lost.

Phillip shakes his head. "Where are you right now?" he asks, bewildered.

"I'm sorry, I just have a lot going on right now. Catherine is having her event, and I was invited, but I don't think I can go now since we are headed to Big Sur," I say.

"We can stop by on our way out," Phillip suggests.

"No, we can go to Big Sur. It's fine."

As we leave Carmel, we drive past Catherine's event. Looking out the window of the car, I see quite a few people, making me wish I had attended.

"Looks like it's a good turn out," says Phillip.

"Yeah, looks like it."

"We can still stop by for a quick second. I really don't mind."

"No, no. It will only delay our trip. Let's just go."

As we turn the corner, I notice Emery, the man I met on the beach the night before. I watch him as he gets out of his car. Upon seeing him clearly, I feel my heart beat fast. He is beautiful. He quickly turns to look in my direction and notices me as well. I smile and wave goodbye as we pass.

"Who's that?" Phillip quickly asks.

I look back to see if Emery is still there, but I can't see him anymore.

"Honey?" Phillip says.

"Oh, sorry. It's the new neighbor. Remember the house that was for sale three houses down from us?"

"No? Wait, the Montgomerys' house? They moved?" Phillip asks, surprised.

"Yes, they did. And quickly too."

"Have you actually *met* this guy? Like, he came over and introduced himself or something?" Phillip asks, probing.

"Last night I went for my usual beach stroll, and he was there. He introduced himself and told me he had moved here just recently."

Phillip turns to look at me, slightly upset. His jealousy is easily triggered. "Why did he feel the need to introduce himself? It's not like it matters."

"What's wrong with him saying hello and introducing himself?" I ask.

"Well, for one, he's not average looking. Two, I don't trust him. And three, I wasn't there," Phillip says with a smirk.

I shake my head and smile at him. "At least you're *honest*."

The book event at Catherine's looks like a success to Emery, judging by the crowd that has already arrived. Right away, Catherine walks straight to him, with Jess beside her.

"I haven't met you yet," Jess says, extending her hand after Catherine introduces them. "Did you come all this way just for the event?"

"Yes and no. I came here for the event, but upon seeing this quaint town, I bought a place and now reside here."

"Oh, I see. What a baller," Jess says, laughing.

Emery sees Catherine give Jess an awkward look, as though admonishing her for referring to his financial situation. Jess takes the hint and changes the subject. "So, Emery, are you married? Single?"

She is shamelessly flirting with him. Catherine glares at her.

"What?" Jess asks, confused. "I can ask . . . right, Emery?" She looks at Emery for approval.

Emery is flattered by her attention but lets her down gently. "I am not available," he says politely.

Jess tosses a quick smile toward Catherine and nods. "I'm sure we'll meet again." Then she excuses herself and heads toward the drinks table.

Catherine quickly pivots. "So, you found my place without a problem?"

"I did. Thank you." He lowers his voice and leans in slightly. "Catherine, I wanted to tell you what happened last night. I met a woman by the name of Rose. I was sitting on the sand enjoying the beach at night, and we introduced ourselves. Turns out, she's my neighbor . . . and she looks exactly like Helena, my past wife!"

Catherine doesn't seem surprised to hear this. "What happened when you talked? Did she seem familiar?"

"Yes, for sure. She looks just like Helena—the way Helena looked when I did my regression with you," Emery says again, even more excited.

"You said her name was Rose?" Catherine asks. "Funny, I do know a woman named Rose. She is a patient of mine. Could we be talking about the same one?"

To Emery, Catherine seems as though she's holding something back, just as she did yesterday, when she helped him with a regression.

"Do you know something you're not telling me?" he asks.

"I believe she is married, if we are talking about the same Rose."

"Married?" Emery asks, disappointed. He can feel his heart deflate.

"Yes, that's right," Catherine says. "In fact, she was supposed to come to this event but canceled last minute."

"Oh, really? What are the odds of that? We would've run into each other again," Emery says, thinking of the possibility.

Catherine nods and glances at her watch. "Oh! It's time. We are going to start undergoing the group regressions. Are you participating?"

As she walks away to the front of the room, Emery nods and follows. He sits beside Jess and closes his eyes as Catherine begins to instruct everyone to close their eyes and relax.

It doesn't take long during the hypnosis before Emery sees himself in the eighteenth century again as Emmett. He is brought to a scene where he and Helena are consummating their love. That was the moment when his infatuation with Helena deepened. The more he got of her, the more he thirsted for her. Their lovemaking was pure ecstasy.

Emery is overcome with all of those emotions for Helena. It is as if something has awakened in him. He doesn't care if she is married in this life; he wants her. After all this time, he has finally found her again, and he'll be damned if he lets her slip through his fingers. She stirs in him desires he simply cannot tame.

He sits there quietly, reliving the memories. His heart is beating faster by the minute.

Catherine continues guiding the class deeper into hypnosis, and Emery can feel she's keeping her attention on him. Surely she knows by the look on his face that he's seeing more than just memories.

Suddenly, Emery is brought to a scene. Rose is there. They're sitting down together at a restaurant, talking. He senses her energy in that moment. She is afraid, secretive, and on edge. Emery tries to calm her, but it doesn't work. He can see her clearly, but he struggles to make sense of it. *Is this a daydream?* he wonders. Maybe it is something that is about to come up? Maybe his subconscious is wishing for it?

Nonetheless, he is taken to another moment, and Rose is standing before him on the beach in a silk floral dress. The look of fear is once again on her face. She is speaking to him, but he can't quite make out what she is saying. It worries him, but he tries to shrug it off.

He comes out of his hypnotized state before anyone else. Emery opens his eyes and immediately turns to look at Catherine.

He indicates that he has something urgent to tell her. Catherine signals for him to wait, because everyone else has just gone under. Emery excuses himself to use the restroom, and as he does, he thinks about what he saw. He tries to remember every detail. He wants to be accurate.

Upon leaving the restroom, he sees some people standing about and talking quietly. Catherine is now sitting beside a woman who has tears streaming down her face. Emery watches from afar, respectfully. Experiencing his own regressions is powerful, but seeing others experience theirs is incredible to watch.

He is eager to speak to Rose and ask her what she knows, to hear what she has seen. Is she aware that they are deeply connected by their past? Has she felt that love from another time resurfacing now? Surely none of this is coincidence—being here, now, in this town, where Rose is also living. Emery wholeheartedly believes that it is fate's design. No one can tell him any different.

One of the participants, a woman, is brought out of hypnosis with a peaceful smile. She looks at Catherine and thanks her. Emery is waiting patiently to approach Catherine, but everyone else is looking to speak to her as well. It feels like a waste of time to wait, so he decides to leave. He'll email Catherine instead.

Grabbing his coat, he heads out and goes home. He drives past Rose's home and glances at it. What a wicked game fate plays, by allowing him to be so close yet with such complex restrictions and barriers between them. The woman he loves lives only three doors down from him. It feels like torture having to sit quietly with what he knows. On the other hand, he doesn't want to scare Rose off with all the information he has. This is too important to mess up with poor timing or miscommunication. Yet he hopes maybe she knows something about their shared past too.

Emery emails Catherine that night and tells her everything he knows, including the new information he obtained from his time at her event. Emery shares the intensity of his emotions, how he struggles to keep his cool. This isn't like him; he is a cool, calm, collected, and charming man. But Helena or Rose upends who he believes himself to be. He divulges how ashamed his past actions make him feel. His dark side—his "shadow self"—being made apparent is hard for him to witness. Emery asks Catherine for guidance on the matter. Has anyone else gone through something similar? He doesn't hold back, letting her know that he would like to speak to Rose and tell her what he knows.

He sits by his fireplace in the living room, contemplating his life. Emery knows in his heart that he can't imagine his life without Rose. He feels torn between his passion for her and his moral code of ethics; after all, she's a married woman. He knows that what he wants—her—goes against his most basic principles, which include honor and fidelity. Yet the power her attraction has over him—without her even knowing it—drives him insane. Emery feels crazy and delusional. Even if Rose decided to be with him, how much is he asking of her? An obsessive inner monologue develops within his head, but his heart doesn't budge. The battle between what his heart and head tell him rages on.

What he doesn't know is that, in the meantime, a little farther south of Carmel down in Big Sur, Rose, too, is consumed with thoughts of Emery. Though she enjoys her time with Phillip, trying her best to be as present as possible during their time there, she finds her thoughts nevertheless always returning to Emery, the man who looks and feels like the one she loved in a lifetime long ago.

A few days later, when Emery opens his email while seated at his desk overlooking the Pacific Ocean, he sees exactly what he was hoping to see: a response from Catherine Jennings. Catherine explains what she knows of Rose and her situation, and she warns Emery to be cautious in his pursuit, considering that Rose is married. She admits that she has been seeing Rose regularly as a patient but says Rose's file is highly confidential. If he wishes to know details, he must ask Rose himself. She apologizes for being short and hopes he understands.

Emery is at a crossroads and needs to decide: Should he pursue Rose, given that she is married? Should he ask her quietly if she's ever learned much about a past life in her regressions with Catherine? It is a delicate situation. He looks out at the seagulls skimming close to the water, looking for food. He decides to go for a walk and clear his mind. Strolling along the beach always helps.

An hour later, on his way back home, he sees Phillip and Rose in their car, heading to their house. He watches Rose as she gets out of the car. She immediately sees him and smiles awkwardly. Emery nods and waves back. Right then, Jess, the woman he met at Catherine's event, pulls into Rose's driveway. She gets out and rushes to hug Rose, and the two chat excitedly.

A light bulb goes off in Emery's head. Upon realizing that Jess and Rose are friends, he knows Jess—who was so curious and flirtatious toward him—just might be an excellent way to enter their social circle. But he will take it slowly.

So Emery hatches a plan to befriend Jess. At his next regression appointment with Catherine, he will ask about Jess, maybe get her contact info, under the pretext of wanting to enroll in her astrology classes. There are no guarantees it will work, but he doesn't need a guarantee; he needs an option, and this is his best option at the moment. Besides, maybe the astrological stuff will be interesting.

In my sleep, I see his face; his essence is haunting. Like a dream within a dream. A vision within a vision. The familiarity of his gaze is warm, and it's almost as though a part of me is found. Without knowing him completely, it is hard to know what he knows. Does he know me? Do I know him at all? Is he who I think he is? Half the time I feel insane with all this new knowledge I have discovered. Who are we to each other?

I lie awake beside Phillip, who is sleeping peacefully. Unable to sleep, I sit outside on the balcony. I decide to email Catherine and ask her if she knows anything about Emery. Maybe she knows him? Or has she just met him? He was at her event, after all. It seems like a high probability that she knows him, and my curiosity needs to be sated, which drives me to ask. But I need to sleep; Phillip has told me he has a surprise planned for tomorrow.

The following morning I receive a text message from Catherine. She doesn't say much, only that she wants to speak to me in person. I tell her we'll be gone all day.

"See me as soon as possible when you get back from your trip," she replies.

Phillip planned a helicopter ride for the day. The drive to the airport is pleasant, besides the obsessive intrusive thoughts about Emery/Emmett—and his blue eyes—that crowd my head. I do my best to push them all to the back of my mind and be in the moment with Phillip. I just fear that there will be a new path unfolding before me that I may or may not have any control over. There are changes taking place within, and I continue to change every day.

Phillip wants to reconnect and put more effort into our relationship, and maybe I should do the same. What does it matter if Emery is Emmett? I am married and should be focused on my husband. However, ever since Emery appeared, there has been an energy shift. I can sense it in my bones.

"Are you ready?" Phillip says to me. "Honey?"

"What?" I say, turning to look at him.

Phillip's face expresses concern. "Is everything all right?"

"Yes! Yes, sorry. I was just thinking about my friend Catherine," I say quickly. "Let's go."

When we get to the airport, our pilot walks over and introduces himself. "Hello, I am Emery," he says to my husband and I joyfully.

What are the odds? I ask myself.

After that moment I begin to see and hear his name everywhere. I can't escape it. Fate's whispering to me, refusing to be ignored. Phillip sees that I am constantly in my head, hardly present with him, even if I try my best. He says it worries him, and he blames himself for putting his work before us. He looks into my eyes, seeking reassurance that we are okay.

I don't think he sees it.

Chapter 14

Jess has agreed to meet up with Emery at Evie's Coffee Shop in downtown Carmel-by-the-Sea. Emery is already waiting at the coffee shop when he sees her walking in from where he sits by the fireplace. Jess looks around quickly and spots Emery, waving hello as she goes to order her coffee. She looks a bit nervous—maybe she really is attracted to him. Nothing he can do about that.

"Hi," she says, setting down her coffee and pulling out a chair.

Emery's eyes meet hers, and he smiles. "Nice to see you again," he says. "You're Catherine's funny friend."

Jess looks bewildered. "You . . . you thought I was funny?"

"It was awkward, but it was funny nonetheless," Emery says, laughing.

Jess nods, her face red. Emery picks up on her embarrassment and changes the subject to put her at ease.

"So, you teach astrology?" he asks.

Jess nods. "Yes, I do! Are you currently learning on your own?"

"Very little. But I want to learn more."

It isn't a total lie, just a partial fib. Jess falls for it and invites him to the next class, having no idea the part she is playing in his scheme to meet Rose. At least, Emery hopes Rose is in Jess's astrology class.

They talk for a couple of hours about Catherine and the event, and even about their own individual regressions. He says he's looking forward to learning about astrology—and his "chart," which she says is the all-important piece—in her next class.

On the day of the class, the students arrive one by one, with Jess eagerly awaiting Emery and Rose. Jess messages Rose to make sure she is coming, and as she does that, Rose walks through the door. Jess's face lights up. Rose looks at her suspiciously.

As Rose takes her seat, Emery walks in. Rose is stunned to see him in class and turns to look at Jess.

"Hi, neighbor," Emery says to Rose and takes the seat next to her.

"Hi."

Jess hands Emery his natal astrological chart and begins to teach the class. "Today's subject is synastry charts."

Emery glances at Rose every now and then. Jess breaks the class up into pairs, and naturally Emery and Rose are paired up.

Everyone is instructed to put their charts together and decipher them. Rose takes the lead and immediately notices several aspects of their charts that stand out to her. Emery and Rose both have Venus conjunct the South Node in their synastry. She can hardly contain her shock.

"So, how long have you been studying astrology?" Emery asks.

Still looking at the chart, she answers, "Not long, but I am a very fast learner. You?"

"Same. Looking to learn more." His eyes remain fixed on Rose the entire time.

"So, what brought you to Carmel-by-the-Sea?" she asks as she continues to study their synastry.

Emery sighs. "Honestly? I think fate brought me here. I don't know how else to say it."

With his words, he finally captures Rose's gaze. "What do you mean by that?" she presses.

"I mean fate, or even destiny, led me here. I have been studying the topic of past lives, and I have studied a lot of research done on hypnosis and regressions. I have had regressions done myself, and I keep seeing the same person from my past." Emery pauses for a moment to let Rose think.

"Who do you see?" She stares at him, utterly spellbound and intrigued.

"You," Emery says simply.

Rose looks stunned. She says nothing, but her face seems to portray deep anguish.

"Have you seen me too?" he asks, observing her reaction.

Rose still struggles to say anything. She was likely not expecting such a direct response.

"Please, say something," Emery says. "I'm eager to know."

But instead of giving him a reply, Rose frantically turns away from him, grabs her belongings, and abruptly leaves the classroom.

"Rose!" Emery calls after her.

His heart is beating hard. Has he scared Rose off with what he admitted about his past life and about seeing her? He is filled with regret and fears losing her forever. This was his one chance to get close to her, to know her, and he has blown it.

"Rose!" he says again.

He watches helplessly, his shaking hand over his heart, as Rose gets into her car and drives off. The pain and fear of another lifetime come rushing back.

Jess walks over to him, concerned. "Emery? What happened? Why did Rose run off like that?"

Emery's eyes tear up with a desolate expression.

He says nothing but goes back in to grab his stuff. Then he drives himself home.

With Emery coming into my life, I can only assume he wants more than friendship. Suddenly, with a flash of insight, I fear things will only grow more intense. Will history repeat itself? Why would destiny want this?

As I lie down on the couch, my heart continues to beat faster and faster, filled with adrenaline. All the memories of the past come rushing in. The past-life regressions are too real. I can't believe Emery confirmed aloud what we both suspected. How is Emery even here, in the same town with me?

Everything was somewhat of a theory until now. All the research, thinking, dissecting, analyzing, and synchronicities were leading up to this moment, all of which overwhelms me. In that classroom, I felt the fear rushing through my veins. How is all of this happening? It feels like too much to take in. The only option I really had in that moment was to run.

I fall asleep on the living room couch almost immediately, and I begin to see new memories from the eighteenth-century lifetime—my life, as Helena, with my beloved Emmett.

The sun is shining brightly on Emmett and me. We are standing in a white rose garden he designed and had made just for me. Emmett walks about the garden, carefully selecting the best rose he can find.

I relive the memory as if I am standing there in that space in time. Looking up to the sky, I close my eyes slowly and inhale deeply. I hear Emmett's voice calling my name—Helena—like a sweet symphony calling me home. Opening my eyes, I see Emmett standing before me, holding the most magnificent white rose I have ever seen. His blue eyes look at me attentively, leaving no further shred of doubt that Emery and Emmett are one and the same. I fully recognize his soul and surrender to fate's desire. On my left hand, I wear an emerald on a dainty gold band. I see it upon taking the rose from Emmett.

Soon after, I awake from my dream at 4:44 a.m., back in the present. I try, but I can't go back to sleep. I decide to walk across the street to the beach. I sit on the sand and recall my dream. I keep awake, reminiscing, until sunrise.

My soul is slowly remembering that time long ago, a love from another time coming back to find me. My soul is reminding me of where I have been. A powerful love ensnares the body, mind, and soul completely, showing up almost as if to tempt me. What will I do? Two paths lie before me, and the choice is up to me.

Fate's whisper will guide us to our rightful paths. Even if we stray too far and drift off, seeking an answer to a question we have right in front of us, we'll get back on the right path. The mind may intervene and try to convince our heart that what it knows is wrong. In the end, our hearts know far more than our minds ever could. We can only ever know the right way to go if we surrender our minds and listen—carefully, attentively—to our heart when it speaks.

This kind of surrendering may be unfamiliar territory for someone who is accustomed to using their mind to rationalize matters of the heart. But matters of the heart are not to figure out, sort, and dissect. They are simply to wholeheartedly *feel*.

I make my way back home and make some coffee. Having had time to think and process, I call Catherine, who schedules me for that afternoon. When driving over to Catherine's, I drive past Emery's home. I don't dare to look.

Catherine is standing at her door when I pull up, her warm smile lighting up her face upon seeing me. She stretches out her arms to give me a big hug.

"I am so relieved to see you!" she says. "You have no idea! I've been so worried about you."

I embrace Catherine back. "I have a lot to tell you. It has been a very interesting past couple of days."

Catherine raises her eyebrows and leads me up to the door. "Yes, I bet! I have spoken to Jess, and she told me her account of the situation."

I walk in and take a seat on the couch. Catherine sits across from me, as usual.

"I don't even know where to begin," I say, looking at Catherine.

"Start wherever you want." She reaches for her notepad and pen and waits on me.

I look down at my wedding ring. "You know Emery, don't you? I believe his last name is Williams?"

"Yes, I do. He is a patient of mine."

"Well, I met him a few weeks ago on the beach and then again in my astrology class. From there, things became a little too much for me to handle."

"I was told by Emery what happened. He called me right after, and we spoke. He told me that he talked to you about his regressions."

I nod nervously. "Yes, he told me that in his regressions, he sees me. I mean, I sort of had a gut feeling that he was Emmett, the man I see in mine. But I wasn't expecting this. I wasn't aware that he knew about any of this! He just dropped it all on me suddenly. I panicked! I didn't know what to say or do, so I just ran out of the room that day."

Catherine jots down notes. "He told me he sat beside you in class, and you were going over charts and had an aspect that sort of validates what these regressions show?"

I nod again. "Yes, and that's when we started talking about past lives, regressions, and what brought him to Carmel-by-the-Sea. That's when he started talking about fate or destiny bringing him here. He said that he kept seeing someone every time. And that led me into asking who, and he flat-out said it was me."

"Okay, so you panicked because he confirmed to you what you suspected, correct?" Catherine asks.

"Yes! Yes, that's exactly it. I mean, I don't know what any of this is supposed to mean. I don't understand. These regressions . . . I mean, I believed that what I was seeing was real. They feel so real. However, having that confirmation is something hard to grasp. I mean, it's real! This is all *real*. It sounds silly, me saying this, but what is life? What is this?"

"Let me ask you this," Catherine says. "What frightens you about this? What are you afraid of?"

I pause for a moment, thinking Catherine's question over, and my eyes begin to water. "I'm afraid of history repeating itself, and I am afraid of what is to come," I finally say, my voice shaking as I speak.

"History repeating itself?" Catherine asks. "What do you mean by that exactly?"

I wipe a tear away from my cheek. "I have an overwhelming sense that I have no choice in the matter, that what is supposed to happen will happen."

Catherine hands me a tissue. "My best advice to you is to let things unfold the way they should. Do nothing. Don't overthink anything. Otherwise, you will drive yourself insane."

I nod in agreement. Catherine's words of advice calm me down.

"Is there more you want to tell me? Or shall we begin?" Catherine asks.

"You said Emery is your patient, right?" I ask.

"Yes, why?" Catherine says, staring at me.

"I want to know about him. What more has he told you? What has he told you about me?" I press further.

Catherine looks down at her notes uncomfortably.

"Rose, if you wish to know more about Emery, I'm afraid you're going to have to talk to him. I can't disclose anything further, especially about our session conversations." Catherine looks at me, still uncomfortable. "I'm sorry. I just can't."

I nervously bounce my leg. "All right. I understand. Let's begin then."

I lie down on the couch and close my eyes. The more regressions I undergo, the easier it is for me to enter into a deep state of relaxation. It feels almost like a muscle getting stronger and stronger each time.

In the scene before me, I am Helena, standing beside Emmett, my husband, at a fancy ball in London being hosted by Emmett's family. Everyone who knows the family has been invited. The ball is grand and lavish. At the party, Emmett's father is to announce his new business partner, a Frenchman everyone can't stop talking about. He is wealthy, incredibly handsome, and very good in business.

I watch as the waiter pours champagne in my glass. At my table, Sir Ashby James excuses himself to go to the stage.

"Good evening to all!" he says. "Thank you for coming. I wanted to take this moment to introduce to you my new business partner, Mr. Pierre Martin!"

Pierre walks up to the stage graciously. His green eyes are gleaming with happiness. He greets Sir Ashby respectfully and says a few words. Looking into the crowd, he spots me and seems to forget what he was about to say. Emmett's keen eye notices Pierre's gaze in our direction, and I can see that makes him feel slightly confused.

Pierre clears his throat and recovers, thanking Sir Ashby for his partnership and friendship.

Soon after, Sir Ashby brings Pierre over to the table to introduce him to us. Pierre's eyes always go back to me, despite the many people at our table. Emmett takes notice and seems displeased by Pierre on the spot.

Sir Ashby leads almost everyone to the dance floor, except Pierre. Emmett and I can see in Pierre's eyes his eagerness to speak to me, but Emmett stays by my side the entire time, making that seem out of the question.

Finally, Pierre walks over to us and says hello. We exchange small talk.

Then Emmett asks Pierre a question that seems to have been burning in his mind ever since he saw Pierre take the stage with his father. "How did you and my father become acquainted?"

"He worked with my mentor Sir Remy Gautier, whom I have worked with since the beginning of my career in the banking business," Pierre says calmly.

"I see," Emmett says, looking back at me. "Funny, I've never seen you before prior to his announcement, or heard anything of this partnership."

Pierre nods. "It was top secret," he says with a smirk.

Emmett stares at him, unamused.

"I prefer to keep my business dealings close to the vest. I'm sure you, of all people, must understand this," Pierre continues.

"I handle my business dealings with great virtue, so I assure you I have no need to," Emmett responds in a stoic fashion. He clearly doesn't like Pierre and gazes at him in the same manner someone would a potential threat.

Pierre looks at Emmett, picking up on his disapproval of him.

Sir Ashby comes to the table to collect Emmett. "I have someone I want you to meet," he says, taking him away quickly. From the looks of it, Sir Ashby is having a really good time.

Displeased and reluctant, Emmett follows his father.

"Care for a dance?" Pierre asks me, seizing the moment.

I look nervously back at him. "Do you deem it appropriate?"

Pierre takes Emmett's seat, opens up a bottle of champagne, and pours himself a glass. "Is your husband the jealous type?" he asks with a grin.

I look to the dance floor without answering him.

He watches me for a few moments, sipping his champagne. Then, getting up from his seat, he leans over to me and extends his hand. "Please?" he asks. "Just one dance?"

Nervously, I oblige.

We make our way to the center of the dance floor and take our place among everyone. The chemistry between us is still there after all these years.

"Are you all right?" Pierre asks, sincerely concerned.

I turn to look at him, caught off guard by his question. "What do you mean?"

"After everything, the way things were left between us. Are you all right?" Pierre asks again.

The memories come flooding in to my mind, incredibly painful to remember. I nod quietly in response to his question.

"Do you have any idea how long I've searched for you," Pierre goes on, "loving you all these years? I was beginning to lose hope, and then, just like that, here you are—like magic."

"Stop," I say, panicking. "That is all in the past now."

But Pierre holds me closer. "Not for me, it isn't. I doubt you've forgotten the love and passion we shared. I promised I'd find you again, and I've kept that promise. You, on the other hand . . . ," he whispers in my ear.

I can feel his resentment.

As Emmett returns to our table, he glimpses the two of us dancing together. I see him sit down, clearly brooding.

"Pierre, Emmett is back at the table. I must leave you early," I say, trying to escape, glancing over at Emmett. Emmett gives me an angry glare.

"The song is almost over," Pierre says, holding on tight to my hand, refusing to let go.

"You are going to cause problems."

"Over a dance? I doubt it," Pierre says, completely unbothered by the situation.

Before the song ends, Emmett walks up to us and grasps my hand. "We are leaving."

I can feel by the nudge that he is quite angry. He leads me through the room, out the grand front doors, and into the chilly night air, where several carriages are waiting.

"Emmett!" Pierre says, following us out to the carriages.

"Get in!" Emmett says to me, opening the door of the carriage. He closes it behind him to confront Pierre. "Your blatant lack of respect for me is dangerous," he tells him angrily.

"I meant no disrespect," Pierre says, trying to calm him.

"Don't play that game with me. I know exactly who you are! Stay away from my wife, or the next time, I won't be so polite," Emmett warns.

Emmett gets into the carriage and begins to interrogate me on the way home.

My heart is crushed. I feel badly about Pierre, and even worse about the way Emmett is behaving. "Stop!" I say. "Why these questions? I have never seen this darker side of you!"

"That was before your former lover decided to walk into town and make advances toward you. Any husband would be upset! Don't try and play it off as if I have no right to feel upset."

Refusing to give the conversation any more traction, I stay quiet. I alight from the carriage quickly upon arriving home and rush to our shared bedroom. Emmett stays in his office, sulking.

I dress in my silk nightgown and go downstairs to Emmett. He is seated in his favorite chair by the fireplace with his glass of brandy, still jealous and brooding.

I stand at the doorway of his office, staring at him. "Still upset?"

He doesn't answer, refusing to look at me. I walk over and stand in front of him, but Emmett refuses to respond or even glance at me.

I proceed to take off my nightgown and let it fall to the floor.

He looks at me, his astonishment giving way to his devilish grin. "What are you doing?" he asks.

"The real question is, what are you doing wasting time?" I quip back.

"What a good question," he replies gently, his gaze now fixed on me. "Please forgive me."

I press my nose against his affectionately and peer into his eyes. "All is forgiven."

Somewhere close by, I hear Catherine's voice fade in softly as she begins counting down.

Before I leave the scene, I can hear Emmett say, "I don't think you know—you don't know how much I love you. I love you so much."

Within seconds, I find myself back in Catherine's office. I slowly open my eyes and, for the first time, find myself missing Emmett.

Chapter 15

Opening my eyes slowly in Catherine's office, I feel slight chills down my spine. The past is all very real, and it is hard to sift through my present feelings and the feelings of the past. Now they all just seem completely merged and slightly murky. I see Catherine's green eyes gaze at me.

"Same time next week?" she asks.

I sit up and nod. "Yes, same time."

Catherine closes her notebook and walks me to her front door.

"Catherine," I say before leaving, "Emery is Emmett, isn't he?"

She nods and smiles warmly.

On my way home, I decide to take the long route. Part of me is still highly critical of all I have experienced and seen thus far. Yet a larger part of me believes it as truth—a truth that has been lying dormant in me, just waiting to be discovered. Half the time I think I must be going crazy. The more I search and discover, the more I sense a shift in me. It's as if I have been living a lie, and suddenly my old life seems stale and outgrown.

Fear courses through my veins. Growth is scary. Change is scary, but only because I don't know what lies ahead. Everyone dreads uncertainty. In the end, I fear whatever I choose will no doubt leave someone hurt—Phillip, Emery, me. But what do I do? When fate keeps whispering, it takes hold of me, refusing to let go.

There is no ignoring the information I know now—that I was in love with Emmett and that I am still in love with him. It is like trying to unsee something. You simply can't; my life is completely changed because of it.

My mind races a mile a minute it seems, so I pull off the road and walk over to a nearby cliffside, enjoying the beautiful view of the ocean. The sensation of the fresh ocean air feels incredible in my lungs. Completely hypnotized by the view, I fail to realize a family has stopped nearby as well. I fall out of my spell when I hear a young boy running over to where I am. His mother calls out his name.

"Emery!" she shouts. "Emery, wait! Don't run off!"

I turn to look at the boy and his mother without saying anything. Then I walk over to my car and leave.

What are the odds? I think to myself.

Driving home as the sun begins to set, I think of Emery. I wonder how much he knows. Has he seen more than I have? He says he remembers me as his wife. Does he still feel the kind of love I feel for him?

The only way to know for sure is to speak to him myself.

But I am too afraid to contact him directly. It just seems inappropriate. I highly doubt his interest in me is strictly platonic or for some sort of research project. Not to sound egotistical, but given our history as husband and wife in the past, I don't think fate is bringing us back together to be best friends.

Pulling into my empty driveway, I see that Phillip isn't home, as usual.

I draw a bath for myself and unwind. There's not much else to do. I recite aloud the thoughts swirling in my head, a habit I've had ever since I was a child. I whisper them to myself without thinking, almost as if channeling someone else's words:

Little breadcrumbs here and there.
Little breadcrumbs everywhere
Little breadcrumbs for me to find.
Little synchronicities all around.
Leading down a predestined road.
Paved for me before I was even born.
Hear my calling and do not be afraid.
For all is shaping out to be as it should.
Life is a winding road, meant to keep you guessing.
Fate's whisper calls out.
Follow me to your destiny.

As I sink into the bubbles and give way to how much I yearn to know more, I decide to fully commit to discovering more. What if this journey takes years? An insatiable desire emerges within me to keep looking, to keep digging. However, I am also torn between that desire and the feeling that it's all wrong and that I would be better off not knowing. Curiosity killed the cat, or so the saying goes.

Down the street, Emery lies in bed thinking of Rose, desperately wanting to know what she is thinking, hoping he hasn't scared her off completely. Every time he thinks of her, his heart begins to race.

She, a complete stranger before now, has a hold on him. But she isn't a stranger, he quickly corrects himself. *I've known her before, and she knows me as well. I just need to hear her confirm it.*

Hours turn into days, and days into weeks.

Emery remains in Carmel-by-the-Sea, hopeful that it won't be too long before Rose finds her way back to him. He figures if fate brought him all this way, it makes no sense to leave things this way. Living a couple doors down—so close but yet so far—doesn't make things any easier. Rose is just out of reach. How cruel can fate be, to taunt him in such a ruthless manner?

He continues seeing Catherine regularly but never bumps into Rose, despite his desperate hope to do so. Several months go by. Emery begins to lose faith, still completely and hopelessly in love. He can't stop thinking about her. All the old memories overwhelm him with a deep love for her, the love he has been looking for his entire life. It finally dawns on him that the roles have switched. Phillip now stands in the position Emery held in the eighteenth century. How twisted.

It's such a wicked price to pay, to now be on the outside looking in. To want someone who is with someone else. To feel the pain and agony of being without. To have all the knowledge and memories he has now of the past, only to suffer in silence in the present.

On a windy Tuesday morning, Emery makes his way up the steps to Catherine's office, unsure if he wants to know anything anymore. What's the point?

The gold knob turns, and the door opens before he can reach it.

There at the door stands Rose.

Emery stops, at a loss for words, completely caught off guard. He trembles slightly while gazing at Rose—at the side of her head. She hasn't quite noticed him yet, as she is still chatting with Catherine. Emery stands and waits quietly.

A moment later, Rose turns to see Emery standing before her. She's clearly stunned.

Before Emery can say anything, Rose says, "Oh! Sorry. I'm leaving." Then she rushes past him.

But Emery quickly turns toward her. "Wait, Rose. Can I speak to you for a second?"

She stops but doesn't turn around. Emery gently reaches for her arm.

Rose finally—but reluctantly—turns to face Emery. She gazes into his eyes.

In her heart, Rose knows she has no choice but to face the truth—the truth her heart has known since the beginning. There, in his gaze, lies her truth. She belongs to him and he to her. Rose has been uncertain about forming any concrete thoughts about fate, destiny, and people's free will to choose. Or is it all one and the same? Do we *create* our destiny? Is fate something we choose? One thing is for certain: She sees her fate in Emery.

"What do you want to talk about?" Rose asks nervously, still entranced with Emery's eyes.

"Us," he answers simply in his deep voice.

Taken aback by his bluntness, Rose hesitates to say anything.

"Please?" he pleads.

Rose nervously nods. "All right."

"Let's take my car," Emery suggests, "if you're comfortable with that?"

"It's fine," she replies, trying to control her nervousness. She is bracing herself for what Emery has to say. It could change everything, having it all laid out bare on the table. No more ambiguity. And Rose knows that a path will have to be chosen.

Emery opens the door of his car for her.

Rose gets in quickly. Her hand trembles as it rests on her leg. Looking out the window of the car, she sees Catherine by the window. They stare at each other, and Catherine nods and gifts Rose a comforting smile. Rose looks down at her hand for a moment and then back at Catherine confidently.

"Ready?" Emery asks.

"Yes."

Emery drives to Big Sur, and the drive, despite the sharp twists and turns, is surprisingly peaceful. Rose's nervousness has completely dissipated.

"Where are you taking us?" she asks.

"To this beautiful little private beach I have just discovered. It's off limits to the general public, but I was granted permission to visit," he says calmly, taking the turns like a Formula One driver. He smirks. "You're not prone to car sickness, are you?"

"If I wasn't before, I am now," Rose quips.

Emery laughs and speeds up. "It's okay. We are almost there."

A few minutes later, Emery finally slows down and pulls over. He turns off the car and runs around to open Rose's door.

"Come on," he says softly, extending his hand for hers.

She places her hand in his and follows him down the path to the beach just below the cliff.

"It is breathtaking here," Rose says, genuinely impressed.

"It is. I love it here. I come often—when I can't stop thinking of you," Emery says in earnest.

The view is wonderful, but the windy and salty sea air is cold against Rose's skin. She grips her coat a little tighter. The sun begins to set. A large rock with a hollow arch allows for the setting sun to peek through, the bright orange color illuminating the sea. It makes the ocean water appear as if there are emeralds on the surface, reflecting the light of the sun. Rose watches a few seagulls fly by; for once the gloomy clouds are nowhere in sight.

She swallows nervously. Emery's openness and honesty are disarming and unexpected. You would never guess that he was afraid of what he felt, or how much he has tried to talk himself out of what his heart feels for Rose. A vicious war raged within him between logic and heart, just as it did with Rose, but he surrendered earlier than she did.

He turns his gaze to her and just observes her, mesmerized by her beauty. "Do you know what I know?" he asks her softly.

Rose looks at him. "Do I know what you know? About us?"

Emery nods.

"I think so," Rose says, her nerves returning a bit.

"We were together in the eighteenth century. We were married, had children, a home. But someone from your past in that life came between us . . . or tried to, anyway," Emery says.

"Pierre Martin," Rose says, stopping Emery in his tracks.

His eyes grow wide, and he moves closer to Rose. "So, you do know everything? Do you know what happened?"

Rose nods. "I was unfaithful. . . . I betrayed you . . . and you killed him," she says, struggling to finish her sentence.

Emery takes Rose's hand in his. "Is it too much to ask how all this has made you feel? What do you think about all this? Because I have to be honest with you—half the time, I thought I was going mad."

"You are not alone in that," Rose says in an uneasy tone.

Emery takes Rose's hand and places it on his chest. "Do you feel how fast my heart is beating? That's because of you. I can't control how I feel for you. I don't want anyone else but you, Rose. And maybe this is wrong. Maybe I shouldn't want you or feel this way for you. But I do, and it's driving me insane! It sounds crazy, but I love you . . ."

Emery pauses for a moment, realizing he has just said what he's been fighting all this time.

"I am so in love with you I don't know what to do with myself," he struggles to say. The power of his feelings scare and overwhelm him.

Rose stares at Emery, unsure of what to say. She can see that he is afraid.

"Dear god, please say something, Rose!" Emery pleads.

"I am just as afraid as you are, believe me," Rose says. "Everything you said about how you feel and the journey you've gone through is a reflection of me. I have seen what you have seen. We have loved each other in other lifetimes, and here we are as if no time has passed. . . . I think fate has been whispering to us both, leading us to each other. This is no coincidence, but we still get to choose."

"Choose?" Emery whispers to himself, nodding and remembering what the guides said to him.

Rose looks at him, confused. "What?"

Emery shakes his head. "Nothing, just thinking aloud."

"When fate calls, I think we still get to choose whether to answer its call or not. Don't you?" Rose asks.

Emery lets out a disappointed sigh. "Yeah," he says simply. "Can I ask you then, what do you choose?"

Rose turns her gaze to the setting sun. "It is too soon to say. I have two paths in front of me, and I can choose to keep my life the way it is now or make a choice that will change my life forever. There is no going back. There is a lot to consider. This isn't a decision that I can just make at the drop of a hat, Emery."

Emery understands completely, although selfishly he wants a straightforward answer. Rose's ambiguous answer leaves him unsatisfied.

"Do I have a chance?" he asks more directly.

"I can't answer that."

"I need to know now if I should try . . . if I at least have a chance? . . . Please say something," Emery presses.

"We can take things slow and see where this goes. Phillip and I are not together anymore. I don't see why we can't explore the possibility of us," Rose says, finally giving a full answer.

Emery smiles as if a huge weight has been lifted off his shoulders. "That's good enough for me."

"Shall we go?" asks Rose. "It's gotten dark so quickly."

"Yes! I was actually going to ask you. Would you like to join me for dinner tonight?"

"Sure," Rose says, happy for the invite.

They go to dinner in the heart of downtown Carmel-by-the-Sea and are seated by a charming box window. The restaurant ambiance is very romantic, with little tea light candles and perfectly selected white roses on every table.

Rose and Emery have now activated both of their destinies by making contact with each other. Suddenly, it becomes clear to Rose that maybe this is what fate wants. The more time she spends with Emery, the more she finds herself being pulled in further. The familiarity of their exchange is incredibly seductive.

People always talk about running away from what fate whispers. They talk about running away from destiny. But how do you run away from this?

If you run away from fate, you'll find yourself running around in circles. You'll run away to end up right back where fate wants you to be. Fate will surely ensnare your heart until you give in. Destiny isn't something you can avoid. No power on Earth can stop what fate has chosen. One chapter closes so another can open. And sometimes, the next chapter is ushered in by someone new.

And all you can do is trust.

Author's Note

I've always had a passion for writing, which has saved me in the most trying of times. When all seemed awry, as I sat in my favorite mauve velvet wingback chair by the large window in my bedroom, observing the lake water before me, the story of Emery and Rose came to me. I'm not much of a romantic myself, but I fell completely in love with their story. The inspiration came from my own quest for self-discovery, as I asked myself the age-old question: What is life about? What more is there that we don't know about?

As a natural seeker and one who is not afraid to upset the status quo, I decided to inject Emery and Rose's love story with the world I was most familiar with—that of mysticism and esoteric knowledge. It is my sincerest hope that everyone loves this story as much as I do and returns for more when I publish the second and third books in the series.

Until next time.

Acknowledgments

I am forever grateful to everyone who became a part of this incredible journey, to all the guides in human form in my life, and to Imelda Marlow, my dearest aunt, who helped introduce me to *The Secret*, by Rhonda Byrne. I didn't know it then, but that would be the first step on my path to learning about spirituality and the mysteries of the universe.

Adrienne Abeyta, an incredible astrologer, provided me with valuable insight into my personal chart with honesty and compassion. Nichole Huntsman, another incredible astrologer, deepened my knowledge of the subject. I thank these ladies for sharing their knowledge and expertise.

I am grateful for Sarah R. Adams, a wonderful beam of light, whom I came across at a time when I needed a guiding light and healing. I thank Roxanne Heibloem for sharing her gifts with me and helping me find the strength to forgive and open my heart to more.

I am grateful for the love of my life, my son, Emmy. I thank Bobby Quance for his assistance and generosity. For my beloved brother Daniel, who was my noble companion through the dark times, and my dear friend Angela I am also grateful.

C. R. C.

I thank everyone at Greenleaf for believing in me and this much-loved story. Special thanks go to David and Elizabeth, my awesome editor, who did incredible work. In addition, I thank Rebecca, Lindsay, Jessica, Kirstin, Mimi, Diana, Amanda, Evelyn, and Tiffany for the parts they played in this incredible adventure!

About the Author

C.R.C. has always had a passion for writing. She truly enjoys the art of storytelling and self-expression through the written word, having complete understanding of the power a story can have to convey a message to people in a fun and entertaining way. Upon visiting the little seaside town of Carmel-by-the-Sea, C.R.C. couldn't help but be inspired by it. She visits it with her family almost twice a year. The rest of the time, she resides in San Diego, California. In her spare time, she enjoys reading astrology charts, another of her many passions, for her family and friends.